Blood Relations

Bernard Feld

Blood Relations

LITTLE, BROWN AND COMPANY
Boston   Toronto

FIRST EDITION

The characters and events portrayed in this book are fictitious. Any
similarities to real persons, living or dead, are purely coincidental and
not intended by the author.

Library of Congress Cataloging-in-Publication Data

Feld, Bernard, 1947–
    Blood relations.

    I. Title.
PS3556.E453B56   1987   813'.54   86-14767
ISBN 0-316-27753-3

HC

Designed by Patricia Girvin Dunbar

*Published simultaneously in Canada
by Little, Brown & Company (Canada) Limited*

PRINTED IN THE UNITED STATES OF AMERICA

For Susanna,
who inspired me from the beginning

Blood Relations

one

I have been to one too many parties that begin with the orchestra playing "Stardust" and end with an unwanted look into the heart of someone's private hell. I have seen one too many stories with my byline above words I don't want to read again. I have awakened once too often with the distorted image of a human shape before my eyes. And I have gotten a little too old to believe that love can save people from the rest of the world — or from themselves.

And yet . . .

The first time I saw such an image was not in a dream.

They had found the body near the end of a badly paved road, a narrow access road that stopped at the mouth of an abandoned mine. Since the spot was secluded, it had become a combination lovers' lane and pleasure alley, a place where the local teenagers came, when they were not drag-racing, to drink beer or smoke dope or get laid. That much I discovered later when the Hueytown cop explained what he was doing there. They'd had some complaints recently, he said, "but never nothing like this business here."

Three police cars were there when I pulled up. One belonged to Hueytown. The other two, a squad car and an unmarked car, were from Birmingham. A couple of cops were standing in the middle of the road having one hell of an argument. The body had been discovered just outside the Birmingham city limits, and the Hueytown police chief had instructed his officer not to let anyone from the city disturb a thing. The detectives — Sgt. Gann was the one I knew — were pulling their hair out while they tried to tell the local cop, who just stood there with his hands clasped over his big belly, that their police jurisdiction went beyond the city limits. Finally the chief radioed back, said he'd talked to the mayor, and the mayor said to cooperate.

The detectives walked over to where the brown army blanket lay in a little heap at the edge of the road. The squad car's headlights were on, and when they lifted the blanket, I saw a slight pink-and-white shape illuminated against the hard graveled earth. I stood about ten feet back. One of the big uniformed policemen partially blocked my view. All I could make out clearly was one unnaturally white leg splayed at an indecent angle; its foot stuck up into the beam of the headlights, glistening like a wet plaster cast. I felt something turn over in the pit of my stomach.

They replaced the army blanket and Sgt. Gann, who had taken charge, walked up to me.

"No matter how many you've seen, this kind is always hard to take."

I nodded in agreement.

He said it was the body of a white female, she was young, and it appeared she had been shot; but they would have to wait for the coroner's report to say for sure. That was all he could tell me now.

"Right," I said. I couldn't think of anything else to say.

Standing behind Gann was the policeman who had found the body. "Found" is probably the wrong word. He had nearly driven his Ford LTD right over it. Now he was looking as pleased with himself as if he'd just caught a black man robbing his own grandmother. He told the sergeant he knew something was funny when he saw her legs stretched out in the road. With a mind like that, he'll probably make lieutenant before too long.

After they had his statement, Gann told the Hueytown cop in rather pointed language that he was no longer needed. The cop looked indignant, but he was too unsure of his position to argue. He piled into his LTD and pulled away like one of the local teenagers laying rubber, the blue light on his roof spinning furiously.

"I reckon he's had his fun for the night," Gann remarked after he'd left.

It was almost midnight, already a few minutes past my deadline. I wasn't going to learn anything else until the coroner got there, and that might be hours.

So it was a relief to get inside my car and drive back up that blacktop road to the main highway. As for what I had just witnessed, it was horrible enough, but I guess the awful thing was that I wasn't overwhelmed by the horror of it. Maybe it was the failure of imagination that sooner or later becomes the habit of a newspaper reporter, but I could not keep before my mind the one crucial fact of the human life at the heart of it. Instead I thought about McDermott on the city desk, and then I wished I hadn't because I knew he would tell me I didn't have much of a story. I wanted to tell him that I was tired and dirty and that I didn't much care whether I had a story or not. But he wasn't there to tell, and instead of turning back toward town, I turned left in the direction of the Hueytown police station.

The highway from Birmingham to Hueytown leads straight past the steel mills — some of the same mills J. P. Morgan put up seventy-five years ago after he had maneuvered U.S. Steel into buying out the Alabama Coal and Iron Company for a fraction of the value of the raw ore in the mines. The mills are at the western end of Jefferson County, and the entire area is pockmarked with coal pits and ore mines, a few still working but most long since abandoned. Everything out there — the towns as well as the earth — is like an open sore, one that has been rubbed raw so many times that it will never close over and heal again. Even at night when the mines and the pits and the quarries are not visible, you can feel them like fissures in the very surface of the darkness; just as you can feel the ghostly silhouettes of the kudzu-covered landscape spreading beyond the road on either side of you.

Now, as I approached, the change the mills had worked upon the land became everywhere thick in the air around me. The entire western sky began to glow a startling metallic pink, the kind of unnatural color found in an Expressionist painting. Gradually it transmuted into bright yellow-orange, and the air became heavy with the familiar sulfurous smell. The mills were having a run. It is a magnificent sight, a beautiful sight in its own way. But I could not helping thinking that the night sky had the color and odor of an inferno, and I wondered just what lay at the end of it.

I got lucky. Or as McDermott would have put it, personal initiative paid off. I pulled up while the cop was still standing out in the parking lot. He recognized me. Before I could ask a question, he said in a sullen voice, "They told me not to say nothing." But he made no move to go inside, just stood there fingering the bullets on his ammo belt. He looked as if he might talk if I just gave him an excuse to. I told him that it was very important I get the whole story, and that I believed he knew things the Birmingham police didn't.

"They didn't want you around, neither," he sneered. But he warmed up to me a little after I told him I wanted readers to understand that he and not Sgt. Gann had discovered the body. He gave me his full name, Hubert Sylvester Poole, spelling the last name to be sure I had it right.

He was a little hesitant at first, but once he got started, it was all I could do to keep up with him. I tried to get everything down exactly as he told it to me, although I later found that most of it was of no use in the story. (Not that people don't want to read the most lurid details. They do, but they like to think they don't, and a family newspaper cannot afford to call into question what its readers believe about themselves.) For me, however, his account is part of a much larger story, and perhaps it will be of some use sooner or later. This is what Officer Poole told me:

It was near the end of my shift, and I was taking a swing down around Sweetheart Road — it's called that not on account of them kids but because that was the name of the mine. Anyway, I thought maybe I'd find me something, maybe throw a scare into some of them durned teenagers. But there wasn't nobody there, just some trash somebody had throwed out in the road. Some folks don't care where they dump their garbage so long's it ain't in their own front yard, and I reckon even that wouldn't disturb 'em too much. That's why it didn't surprise me none at first. I rounded a curve and come to a stop a few feet in front of it. It looked like one of them plastic dummies you see in a department store window. And I says to myself, "Why in hell would anybody want to leave one of them blamed things way out here?" All I could see was part of the hips and those two legs sticking straight out, so I thought maybe that was all there was to it and that's why they threw it away. But something made me get out of the car, and as I come toward it I begun to get this funny feeling. Then I knew. I knew when I saw her toes. They was painted burnt orange — my wife uses a shade just like that — and some of the polish was chipped away. I pulled the grass back and sure enough there she was laying flat on her back with her arms flung out above her head on either side. All she had on was that little pink top and there wasn't much of that, wrenched like it was clear up over her shoulders. (A pair of blue jeans, sandals, and underclothing were discovered later in the woods a little way off.) She didn't look like she could be much more than about seventeen. Her tits were as hard as prickly pears and they was pointing right up at me. I finally bent down and touched her — and by God if she wasn't still warm. That set me to looking for a pulse, but a'course I didn't expect to find none. Not with her eyes staring like that, and her mouth had a look like she didn't know whether to laugh or cry. Like I say, there was what looked to be a bullet hole down low in her belly where it probably didn't do that much harm, but it didn't do her no good neither. But there was a bigger hole right under her left tit, and I figured that was the one that finished her.

After Poole had given me his statement, I called in from the station to tell them what I had. When I got back, they had been holding the final edition for over an hour. McDermott stood behind me, going over my copy almost before I could get it out of the typewriter and shooting it upstairs.

By the time I got home, the clock on the kitchen counter said five minutes past two. But it seemed much later to me. I forced myself to take a shower before I fell into bed. I was dirty and I still had the faint smell of sulfur in my nostrils. Even after I had showered, I could feel little tremors across my body, as if something unclean was beneath my skin and I couldn't wash it away.

two

*F*or me the real story did not begin in Birmingham at all; it began the winter before in New York City. It was there that I first came to know Cassie Fairchild. She was finishing up at Bryn Mawr; I was in my first year of journalism at Columbia. We met through a mutual friend — a girl I dated who had been two years ahead of her at Bryn Mawr. The girl was from Long Island and Cassie's may have been the first southern accent she had ever heard. And she was so struck by the idea that we were both from Ala*b*ama that she insisted we must meet.

So Cassie and I became friends in an odd sort of way. We discovered we had mutual acquaintances in Birmingham, and there grew up between us the intimacy peculiar to strangers in a foreign place who are able to speak reassuringly of familiar landmarks.

There was nothing romantic about it; at the time I was very much preoccupied with Fran, my Long Island girl. Fran had given me to understand that Cassie was considered beautiful, glamorous even, by Bryn Mawr standards. But whenever I saw her, she seemed to take pains not to appear so; she wore baggy jeans, loose-fitting shirts, and no makeup or lipstick at all. Gradually I came to understand, without her actually saying so, that this was a kind of compliment. It was as if she were saying: "They may think me beautiful, but no one here will ever know me. You see me more as I really am." Even that, however, may have been a pose. As I look back it is difficult to know for sure. I heard also a few vague wild stories about her — there was one about the son of a South American general who wanted to fly her home to meet his parents. I had no idea whether or not the stories were true.

After a time we became confidants. She would tell me about the preppies she dated from Princeton or the Marxists from Fifth Avenue who took her to SWP meetings. And I told her about the Barnard girls from Connecticut who wore their long blond hair down to the patched rear ends of their faded jeans, or about the large-breasted Jewish princesses from Long Island.

Once, when we were having a drink in a bar near Columbia, she narrowed her eyes and asked, "What are you doing up here anyway?"

Sometimes I'd asked myself the same question. After college I had traveled some, worked for a year on a midwestern newspaper. I hadn't lived in Birmingham since I was seventeen, the year after my father died, and I think I had come to New York partly because of him. He, too, had studied journalism at Columbia. Afterward he went to Vicksburg, Mississippi, where his father had once owned land, and joined what was then the most liberal newspaper in the state, eventually becoming editor.

I had come to New York also because I had the idea that I was lacking in a certain kind of experience. I wanted to become, as my father would have put it, "a citizen of the civilized world." Part of this I told Cassie over the course of a few more drinks. When I had finished, she laughed and asked, in the same low voice, "Well, have you?"

"Have I what?"

"Become a citizen of the civilized world."

I had the feeling she was still laughing and I didn't reply. She gave me a long look and her eyes narrowed even more. "When are you going to go back home?" she asked.

At the time I had no answer for that either. And soon afterward I lost touch with Cassie. I called the school several times, but she never called back. Later someone told me she had left Bryn Mawr. I wondered if she had gone to South America after all.

That spring I began to feel a restlessness I couldn't define. I signed up for courses in journalism, literature, and philosophy, and managed to neglect all of them equally. Finally, after a disagreement with a Columbia dean over some sort of principle, I made up my mind to leave school and head back south. Maybe the principle was no more than homesickness. At any rate, one balmy April evening I stood at the windswept corner of 116th Street, holding two calfskin suitcases that had been my father's, hailing a cab for La Guardia.

As you approach Birmingham from the air, you see a long low ridge that lifts itself like a clumsy prehistoric creature out of the landscape of mines and mills and rain-filled quarries from which the city grew. To anyone familiar with the icy walls of the Rockies or the majestic Adirondacks, this ridge is scarcely more than a gentle incline, the most modest beginning of the Appalachian foothills. Red Mountain, as it is called, is both symbol and substance of the city, a mound of iron ore that gave rise to Birmingham's industrial prominence in the late nineteenth century. It is a rich honeycomb of now abandoned ore and coal mines, and nestled against its side, like fortresses, are the Tudor mansions and imitation Italian villas of the families who used to own the coal mines and ironworks — overlooking the rest of the city from a comfortable height. Looming above it all is the colossal statue of Vulcan, grim-faced god of the forge, cast from Birmingham iron. He is clad only in a loincloth, and his cast-iron buttocks have withstood assaults from legions of decent Baptist-minded citizenry. Still, he is a convenient symbol for local industry. And no one seems to mind that Vulcan was the ugliest of the gods and, as the husband of Venus, the greatest cuckold among them.

At first I felt more out of place in Birmingham than in New York — it is easier to be a stranger in a strange city than in a familiar one. On the street the occasional ghost of an old acquaintance stared after me as if I myself were the ghost. Everything about the place seemed a little out of focus, like a familiar landscape seen in a dream.

But the more I saw of Birmingham, the more it seemed that it was not the city that was out of focus but me. I had forgotten the almost explosive luxuriance of the southern spring. The air was thick with the fragrance of honeysuckle and wisteria. The kudzu flourished everywhere. In the suburbs swimming pools were being cleaned; the afternoons began to lengthen into gin and tonics. And the University of Alabama was in the middle of spring training — the talk was that they were flush with running backs and had a good shot at Notre Dame next season.

For a couple of weeks I drifted through the warm spring air as aimlessly as milkweed. I loafed around the Elite Cafe, where you could still get beer and barbecued ribs for under three dollars. And I called a few people. But after I had listened to an old fishing companion discuss the booming market for bathroom fixtures and seen a girlfriend looking twenty pounds heavier and two husbands older, I stopped doing that. I moved into one of the city's old neighborhoods, at the base of Red Mountain, on the other side of town from where I had grown up. The area, called Highland Park, had been laid out by Frederick Olmsted, the great American landscape architect of the nineteenth century. And if you looked closely at the natural contours, the great outcroppings of iron ore, you might see a hint of the more urbane wilderness of Central Park.

I got a job on the *Birmingham Examiner*. The editor had known my father slightly and had admired him, although his own brand of journalism was more pragmatic. At any rate, he was impressed by the fact I'd attended Columbia, even if I hadn't finished. They put me to work on the city side, doing a little reporting and a lot of obituaries. Usually I didn't have to be at work until one in the afternoon. I could eat a leisurely breakfast and read a couple of newspapers. There is something satisfying about a daily newspaper. The sentences are short and easy to read. You can take in the main ideas at a glance. And the papers remain uncluttered by any real complexity or moral dilemma.

When I walked into the city room, McDermott, the city editor, would barely look up. For a man whose business was putting out words, he was peculiarly taciturn. He usually spoke in monosyllables and the only advice he ever gave me was this: "Twenty-two words, Phillips. No sentences longer than twenty-two words."

"What about James Reston?" I asked.

"A hack," he replied. "Look at Hemingway."

Usually all he said when I came in was "Obits piling up." But even writing obituaries is not the depressing business you might think. For one thing, they all follow a regular formula — a ritual, if you will. Obituaries are predictable and in their own way reassuring. And they always end with a list of the survivors, a ready testament to the continuity of life.

Perhaps it was natural that I should progress from obituary writing to police reporting. Each in its own way, it seemed to me, was an attempt to redeem life from random violence and brutality.

The *Examiner*'s regular police reporter was Mike Stankey,

a stumpy man with fierce, reddish gray hair that looked like rusty barbed wire. He'd had the job for fifteen years and he knew practically every man in the police department by his first name. He worked with them, and he palled around with them, and he drank with them. But he drank with anybody or nobody, and some days his hands shook so badly that he couldn't keep them on the typewriter keys. So I began taking care of routine things: robberies, drug busts, domestic shootings. I even worked with Stankey on a couple of page-one stories. And through him I came to be on good terms with some of the detectives.

After I had learned the police beat, I was handed the dubious honor of taking over the graveyard shift two or three nights a week. I spent many of my evenings that summer at City Hall alone in the seventh-floor pressroom, listening idly to the police radio, its staccato bursts of static occasionally punctuated by an intelligible human voice. Most of it was routine. To break the monotony I took along a couple of newspapers and sometimes a book. From time to time I would go downstairs and check with the detectives on duty. Usually if anything did turn up, I would simply coax a couple of paragraphs out of the pre–World War II Royal in the pressroom, then dictate it over the phone.

I began to get comfortable — with the job and with the life. Only one thing disturbed me a little. From the time I had stepped off the plane from La Guardia, the idea of Cassie had been lodged like a tiny irritating pearl at the back of my mind. I was not sure just why, because, as I said, there had been nothing romantic between us. Perhaps because of what she said about going home, the act of returning to Birmingham seemed inextricably bound up with her.

I had no idea, of course, whether or not she was even in Birmingham. And I went about trying to find out by the most indirect means possible. If we did meet here, it would no longer be as two southerners stranded in New York. And maybe I was a little nervous as to just what footing our meeting would be upon. I made some discreet inquiries and found out the reason she had left Bryn Mawr. She'd had some sort of breakdown and spent four months in a place on the coast of Maine. Someone said she had gone to Greece. I even heard she was engaged to a Texas oil millionaire whose daddy owned part of the Dallas Cowboys. After that I left off inquiring altogether.

All that changed one Thursday afternoon in early June. I had most of that day off since I was scheduled to work the graveyard shift that night. I was coming out of the grocery store with a steak and a bottle of Gallo under my arm when someone called my name. I knew the voice before I looked around.

There was Cassie looking just as I'd seen her last, wearing the same oversized red-and-white gingham shirt. "I knew you'd get tired of those Yankees and come back to us," she said.

I was touched by the way she said it, although there was a suggestion of secret amusement in her voice. I saw also that her face seemed a little thinner and in some way softer. But it had a healthy color to it, as if she'd spent the last few weeks playing tennis or horseback riding.

"When did you get back?" she asked me.

I told her and she said, "I wonder if you've tried to get in touch with me."

I said that was an odd way to put a question.

She seemed a little self-conscious. "What I mean is you probably wouldn't have been able to reach me. But I'd like to think you tried."

I said I had tried, without going into details. I asked her where she was living.

"At my parents'. Mostly," she added.

"Well, how is —" I wasn't quite sure how to finish the sentence — "everyone at home?"

"Just the same," she replied breezily. "Mother is still the Madame de Staël of Birmingham and Genghis Khan around the house. And Daddy," she said meaningfully, "has a new friend."

We went next door and had a cup of coffee. I let her know that I had learned the circumstances of her leaving Bryn Mawr.

"I thought about calling you last winter before I left school," she told me. "I really did. But I wasn't in much shape to talk to anyone."

That was about all she said about it except for her brief description of the place in Maine: "Very progressive. Big on crafts. I spent lots of time learning to make silver jewelry, really tacky stuff," she laughed. "It's supposed to keep your mind off suicide."

When we walked outside, I said, "Give me your phone number. We'll have dinner one night."

She hesitated. "Let me call *you*. You'd have a hard time reaching me. I'm sort of — between places. And I may be out of town for the next few days."

I wanted to ask if everything was all right, but that sounded trite so I didn't. Instead I gave her my number at the *Examiner* and told her to leave a message if I wasn't in.

three

*T*he morning after the Hueytown murder, I slept late. But it was a restless sleep, the kind you wake up from feeling like you've been worked over.

I took another shower. Then I went outside and bought a newspaper. I left the paper folded on the kitchen table while I had my first cup of coffee. Halfway through the second cup, I opened it up.

The story was in the bottom left-hand corner of the front page, one column with the headline stacked:

BODY FOUND NEAR
OLD HUEYTOWN MINE
by Nick Phillips

The partially clad body of an unidentified woman was discovered last night near an abandoned mine at the edge of Hueytown.

The victim appeared to have been shot, according to Birmingham Det. Arthur Gann. However, police are awaiting the coroner's report to determine the exact cause of death.

There were another six paragraphs to the story, most of it continued to page twelve. I read through it quickly, then changed clothes and got ready for work.

McDermott didn't say a word when I walked in. I don't

know what it was I expected him to say, but I was faintly disappointed.

Henry Slidell said something, however. Henry Slidell is the religious editor and derives a good deal of satisfaction from the fact that ministers of the gospel are constantly seeking him out. He is forty-five years old, he lives with his mother, and he keeps in the right-hand drawer of his desk beneath a stack of makeup sheets a fair selection of every pornographic magazine sold in Birmingham.

He has a high grating voice, and it sent a shiver up my spine when he said, just above my ear, "I hear you fell into a big story last night, Phillips."

I said something and pretended to be completely absorbed in the obituary I was typing.

"A terrible thing," he went on, "that girl being murdered like that."

This time I didn't say a word, but he continued.

"They said she was shot two or three times, didn't they?"

At that moment Bob Hurlbut, a City Hall reporter whom I had an occasional drink with, stopped on the other side of me. "What's the matter, Henry," Hurlbut asked, "didn't we give you enough of the intimate details?"

Slidell tried to ignore that.

"Come on, Nick," Hurlbut said, "level with us. Did you get a look at the firm young body?"

I felt the hair prickle on the back of my neck. "Go to hell," I said to both of them.

Hurlbut pretended to look hurt. "I just ask 'cause Henry's too bashful to say anything. He was wondering if you could get him a full-color photo to run on the church page — the wages of sin and all."

Slidell turned purple and started sputtering in that high voice. I was relieved when I heard McDermott calling me.

"You're staying on top of this murder business, aren't you?"

"Yeah," I told him.

"Well, get over to City Hall and see if you can find out something new for the follow-up." And as I started out, he shouted after me, "See if she was raped."

The police detectives' squad room was empty except for Lt. O. C. Harris, who was sitting on the edge of his desk paring his fingernails with a pocketknife.

"How's it going?" I asked.

"I'd rather be fishing," he answered, "but I can't complain."

Most of the detectives I had run into tried to appear businesslike and a little brusque, especially in the middle of an investigation. Harris, however, projected the image of a good old boy. But beneath it all he is a decent judge of men and, in his own way, a learned man (he can speak knowledgeably about the more violent of Shakespeare's history plays), and he knows that I know it.

"I need some information," I told him straight out.

"Who don't. You want to know which dog to put your money on, or how to heal an aching heart, or maybe you just need to know where you can get you a little piece once in a while without your old lady finding out. Ask Detective O. C. Harris, you've come to the right place."

"I need to know about that girl they found last night."

"Like to oblige but I can't tell you much."

"Why not?"

"Don't know much," he said. "And most of what I do know's official po-lice business."

My disappointment must have showed, because he said, "Cheer up. I got one little surprise for you."

"What do you mean?"

"I mean that girl didn't die of no lead poisoning."

"She wasn't shot?"

"That's not what I said." He located a manila envelope in a pile on his desk, opened it, and thumbed through the contents.

It was the autopsy report. The police were keeping it under wraps for the time being, but he read me an excerpt. The girl had been shot all right. But that wasn't listed as the cause of death. There were bruises on her chest, and her rib cage on one side had been completely crushed, puncturing a lung and causing massive internal bleeding. According to the coroner, she had bled to death before she was shot.

"Somebody just shot her for fun, I guess," Harris said.

I asked if they had identified her yet.

"Nope. But I'll tell you what I think. I think she's a local girl."

I have noticed that whenever the police speak about a murder victim, they invariably use the present tense.

"What makes you think that?"

"Well, she just don't look to me like a runaway. They're kinda scruffy, you know, hair under the armpits and all. But not this one. She was clean as a whistle." He whistled himself. "Nice legs, too — freshly shaved."

"Thanks," I said, "but I don't think we can print that."

He laughed. "Well, tell it to McDermott. I bet he'd like to know."

I wrote the story quickly, and McDermott sent it up marked ALL EDITIONS. The rest of the day was slow; nothing came in except a few obituaries. There was one about a ninety-six-year-old man who'd fought in World War I and had had six wives. It took me four hours to verify the names of the twenty-eight survivors.

four

Just beyond Red Mountain, five minutes from the city, in a secluded valley created by the Black Warrior River, lies the suburban community of Shady Vale. It is a bedroom community, with miles of fenced and manicured lawns, a village with buildings in the Old English style, even bicycle lanes provided by an enlightened public-works department. Shady Vale has its own mayor and town council, a progressive school system, and a polite but efficient police force to which much of the town is intimately connected by means of electronic security systems. The townspeople also point with pride to the multitude of fine old oaks and stately elms, which they say gave the town its name — although historians maintain that the area was once inhabited by Creek Indians, who left behind a number of burial mounds and called the place "Valley of the Shades." But the Indians have long since been forgotten, their graves bulldozed and then buried again beneath miles of zoysia.

So Shady Vale is a kind of kingdom to itself. It is said to number one millionaire for every seven-two people, and there are probably many who, even if they cannot go through the eye of a needle or enter into the kingdom of God, are content to pass their days here.

But in many important ways Shady Vale is more Birmingham than Birmingham itself. Outside of the few families like Cassie's, who still maintain their ancestral homes on Red Mountain, it is the people of Shady Vale who run things in the city. The community was built in the twenties by the sons of the industrialists and bankers who sixty years earlier had built Birmingham. They had simply put a mountain between themselves and the heart of the city so that the air they breathed did not smell so distinctly of sulfur and they did not have to skim the particulates off the surface of their swimming pools every summer morning.

The main measure of success in Birmingham is a home in Shady Vale. And over the years the town has grown to make room for all sorts of successful people: blunt-spoken businessmen who have worked hard to move their families "over the mountain," corporate lawyers, life insurance salesmen, funeral parlor owners, a Baptist minister whose television show is popular in ten states, even one young man I went to high school with, now "retired" from the drug-dealing business. My own parents once owned a house in Shady Vale. It was on a subdivision-like lot that had been unincorporated when they moved in. They bought the house a few years before I went to college, so I did not spend much time in it. And I do not believe my family ever really felt at home there. But those who live in the subdivisions, as they are called, are not invited to the best parties, nor their sons and daughters to the special cotillions, nor their children to the proper nursery school. There are hierarchies within Shady Vale itself rather like the hierarchies of the angels, or the circles of another place.

I was at work one afternoon about a week after I had driven out to Hueytown, and Shady Vale was as far from my mind as the Sahara, when Cassie called. The call surprised me a little. Maybe I hadn't really expected to hear from her.

She asked if I would mind taking her to the Shady Vale

Country Club. She said her cousin's debut was that Saturday night, that it would probably be a dreary affair and she didn't much care for this cousin anyway, but she ought to put in an appearance. The note of condescension in her voice puzzled me a little; it did not quite ring true. But I wanted to see her again, and I was flattered she had asked me, so I agreed to go.

"You know how to get to my parents' house, don't you?"

I had never been there, but I knew where it was. I guess nearly everyone in town knew that house.

"You can't miss it," she said lightly. "It's the house with fourteen chimneys and I'll keep a candle burning in the tower window."

I hadn't realized how imposing the place was until I swung my car through the stone gate and the headlights pointed up the sweeping brick drive. It wasn't much of an exaggeration about the chimneys. The house was built of pinkish-gray Alabama granite, and it loomed above the highest point of the mountain of iron ore that overlooked the city. It had been put up by Cassie's great-grandfather in the early 1900s in a style that was at best eclectic: The narrow leaded windows just beneath the slate roof looked medieval; but you saw touches of Renaissance Italian in the friezes above the door and the first-floor windows. Inside, I later discovered, there was a cavernous hall downstairs with tapestried stone walls and a thirty-foot vaulted ceiling, while upstairs the main living rooms were evidently intended to call up something of the elegance of the court of Louis XIV.

But the dominant tone, if there was one, was naive English Tudor. The front door seemed fifteen feet high and was of solid oak. When I pressed the doorbell, I heard what might have been a full carillon of chimes echoing somewhere deep inside the house. No one answered at first, and I stood on

23

the stone steps growing a little warm inside my rented tuxedo. Finally I heard a metal bolt being shot back, and the door swung open. A maid in uniform was there to greet me. That is probably an exaggeration. She eyed me as if she thought I might be selling burial insurance. But she had evidently been led to expect someone, and she said, without much enthusiasm, "Miss Cassie be down in a few minutes."

The entrance hall was of pinkish granite like the outside. The maid led me into another smaller hallway and then through the palace of Versailles and into a dark paneled room at the end of one wing. It had a rough stone fireplace and ruby glass windows, but the books that lined the walls nearly to the ceiling gave it a human dimension most of the house lacked. The maid left me standing in the middle of the floor. I felt uncomfortably alone, and I was about to pull a book off the shelf when I suddenly realized I was not alone at all. Sitting far back in a darkened corner, in a deep burgundy leather armchair, was a man who appeared to be half-asleep with a book turned down on his lap. But as soon as I saw him, he looked up and met my glance and I was sure he had been observing me since I first entered. His hair was graying a little, and his eyes were deep-set in a face that was tanned and weather-beaten and that you would have expected to see on someone who spent most of his time outdoors — a sports-man or, better still, an old-fashioned nineteenth-century woodsman. This was Cassie's father. He looked formidable even sitting down, and when he stood to shake hands I guessed he was about six foot two, although it was difficult to tell because he had a way of inclining his head slightly forward as if he were perpetually stepping into some room that wouldn't quite accommodate him.

Cassie had evidently told him a little about me, and he asked what I had studied at Columbia. He spoke in a voice that was scarcely more than a grumble, and I had to strain to understand him.

"A little journalism," I answered, "and a little philosophy, and a little literature."

Mr. Fairchild gave a faint half smile and said, "That most limited of all specialists, a humanist."

"I'm even more limited than that," I replied. "I'm a newspaper reporter."

He seemed pleased at that. I believe he approved of anyone who had a capacity for appreciating the irony of a situation. At that moment we were interrupted by the maid, who reappeared at the doorway and now contemplated the two of us with the same air of misgiving she had shown me earlier.

"What is it, Viola?" Mr. Fairchild asked.

Cassie was ready, Viola announced to us, then gave a barely perceptible shrug of her shoulders that seemed to express her misgivings over the world in general and went out.

I was about to shake hands with Mr. Fairchild before leaving, but he placed one large hand lightly on my shoulder as if to steer me in the right direction and together we walked back to the front of the house.

We stopped in the front hall through which I had entered. Pink granite walls notwithstanding, it was a gloomy place — dimly lit, at least twenty feet wide and probably twice as long, although its length seemed to fade into indeterminate shadows. But into its center swept a dazzling white marble staircase, and suddenly, down that staircase, came Cassie. I had never seen her before dressed in anything other than her blue jeans and shapeless man-sized shirts, and now when she appeared it nearly took my breath away. She wore a black sequined dress cut low enough in front and stretched superbly across her hips. Rising out of the black dress her neck and shoulders seemed as fair and luminous as the marble stairs behind her, and her fine red hair in elaborate curls stood out from her head like a halo. She wore no jewelry at all except for one large amethyst ring, and she carried a small mother-of-pearl handbag that dangled from her wrist by a slender silver chain.

At the bottom of the stairs she stopped for a moment and stood still, looking almost awkward, as though she were truly surprised at finding herself dressed like that. Then she walked up to her father and stretched her neck and kissed him on the cheek, and for an instant I had the impression that they were both in costume for some fancy dress ball and that behind their masks they were smiling wryly at one another. But then she smiled at me and said, "All ready to go?"

I grasped the brass handle of the great oak door and it swung, surprising me, light and easy on its hinges. Together Cassie and I stepped out into the moist, moonlit Alabama night.

When we were in the car, heading over the mountain toward the country club, Cassie said, "Daddy likes you."

"How do you know that?" I asked.

"I can just tell," she said. "He and I are very much alike." Then she added, "Sometimes I think he's schizophrenic."

I started to ask what she meant by that. But she was looking straight ahead out the window toward the waxing moon that hung just above the horizon like a porcelain globe suspended over Shady Vale, and I didn't say anything.

Shady Vale Country Club's official name was The Country Club of Birmingham, although no one called it by that anymore. The original location had been inside the city limits; when Shady Vale was built its members had simply moved the country club over the mountain. But the old name was still accurate because the club remained the social and hierarchical hub of the city.

The building itself was supposed to resemble an antebellum

26

plantation house, but it looked more like a 1930s movie set. Inside were dining rooms and ballrooms and grand ballrooms, a pro shop, a men's bar and grill, even a ladies' tearoom with a mother-of-pearl piano in one corner and, in an enormous white cage, two birds of paradise that seemed to be on the point of molting.

I pulled up beneath the white-columned portico — actually a carport — and an attendant in full gold-braided livery opened the car doors for us. The crowd inside were mostly younger than we were. The men stood in small groups looking cocky but a little uncomfortable, as if they would have felt more at home at a football game or standing around a pinball machine in tennis shoes with Dixie cups full of beer in their hands. Their dates swept across the floor in cream- and peach-colored full-length gowns held up by almost invisible straps or by sheer willpower alone, while their elaborate hairdos were already beginning to give way. Some of these girls wore a sleepy expression, their faces tilted toward the ceiling and eyes only half-opened, as if all their lives they had been exquisitely bored. They looked as if secretly they knew nothing would ever interest or arouse them again, but at the same time they would be willing to try anything, just anything. Perhaps that is what it means to be a debutante.

In the main ballroom a frenzied group of dancers was frozen beneath a strobe light while a band called Dynamite exploded into hard rock. From somewhere else in the building I thought I could hear a string quartet barely contending against them, but it sounded so far off that it might have been a distant car radio.

Most of the party, however, seemed to be jammed into a room off the main ballroom that contained an elaborate crystal chandelier hanging above a very small, overworked circular bar. I wedged myself through to try to order drinks. There were a half dozen bartenders, each pouring liquor deftly out of a bottle in either hand; even so, they were surrounded by such a crowd of empty glasses and anxious faces that I decided I could wait.

I had to hunt for Cassie; I found her talking to a couple who looked about our age. "Mama didn't actually say so," Cassie was telling them, "but she strongly hinted it would disgrace the whole family and probably ruin Daddy if I didn't come."

The girl looked at her doubtfully. "How could you not have come?" she asked.

Cassie introduced me. They were almost newlyweds. Lucy was a striking blond who, after you had looked at her for a moment, just missed actually being pretty. "Don't you just love the band?" she said to me.

"Mama had Benny Goodman at my debut," Cassie remarked absently.

Lucy's husband was Mitch. "Glad to meet you, Phillips," he said. He was the sort of person who could call you by your last name and manage to sound amiably masculine instead of stuffy. "I've read some of your pieces, especially the one on the Tombigbee River project. Sheer pork barrel. Do you think they can stop it?"

"I doubt it. There's too much money pushing behind it."

"Pity," he said. "They're going to lose a lot of prime bottomland; first-rate hunting and fishing, too. I shot my first buck on that river. Never forget it. Flat on my stomach in a swamp for four hours. Trees down there wider than a locomotive, centuries old."

Lucy broke in, tugging at his arm. "Come dance with me," she said.

"Catch you later," said Mitch.

"They've been married three months. I grew up with Lucy," Cassie told me. "Her father's vice-president of First Birmingham Trust and her grandfather is chairman of the board. Lucy's father told Daddy once," — and she mimicked the kind of southern accent peculiar to successful business-men — "'You know I got me a big office down there; got me a big mahogany desk with an appointment book just laying on it full of appointments. Nevuh go down there, nevuh see a one of 'em. Spend all my time on the golf course. It's the best damn way to make money.'" She laughed. "Mitch is going into the bank, too."

"I hope he can play golf," I said.

"Oh, Mitch," she said. "Mitch can play any game he has to."

We ran into other couples, some of them older, friends of Cassie's parents. As we were heading outside, one couple stopped us and were enormously polite although it was ap-parent they were having a ferocious argument. She kept hiss-ing at him in a not-quite-sober voice: "I *knew* this would happen. I don't have to stand for it."

"Save it," the man said under his breath. "Just save that until we get home."

When they had left, Cassie gave me a look that was almost triumphant and said, "My cousin's parents, the parents of the debutante," as if that were the climactic point of an argument she had been carrying on all evening.

"Let's get some fresh air," I said.

We walked out by the pool. The music I had thought I heard earlier was coming from out here — a piano, two fid-dles, and a bass, four middle-aged black men in silver tux-edos. It was humid for early summer, and the music seemed to wander like a desultory breeze through the thick night air. Beneath the high diving board a boy was trying to coax his date and another couple into shedding their clothes and going in. The other girl's date snickered, but the girls themselves remained unmoved. Except for them and one or two other stray couples, we had the place pretty much to ourselves. I turned gravely to Cassie, bowed low, and asked, "May I have this dance?"

"I'll have to check my ca-ahd, suh," she said.

We danced two slow dances in an empty corner of the concrete deck beside the pool. Cassie seemed scarcely to move, but her sequined dress felt as if it were electric beneath my fingers.

"Are you hot?" I asked. I could see tiny drops of perspiration glistening like diamonds against her skin.

"Of course not," she said. "Southern belles don't sweat."

"Well, I do. Let's go inside and get a drink."

Back in the ballroom the band was still giving off staccato bursts of music. We walked across the dance floor and, before we could get to the bar, ran into Mitch and Lucy.

"Listen," Mitch said. "There's nothing going on here. I've got a terrific idea. We'll all go down to the Bluebird Club. They've got an old black man who plays a marvelous jazz sax."

As we left the country club, Mitch told us about the sax player. His name was Ben Tiner, and he had been born in Birmingham but had left years ago. "He's been with all the really big bands: Duke Ellington, Count Basie — you name it, he's played with them."

We got into my car and followed Mitch and Lucy back over the mountain. They had a little Fiat convertible and they gunned it through town, honking and shouting as if they were uproariously drunk and simply couldn't help themselves. For a couple of blocks Lucy even rode perched on the back of the car, waving her yellow slippers in one hand and holding on with the other, although when we met up with them outside the club, she seemed so chagrined at having made a spectacle of herself that she hardly spoke even a word for the rest of the evening.

Mitch went in first. "They know me here," he said.

The Bluebird Club was on the edge of the black business district. But about a third of the clientele on any given night would be white — liberal-minded local people who believed they would hear better blues or jazz because the club was black, and salesmen out for a good time — and the whites were tolerated if not encouraged. Tonight the club was only half-filled, but we waited until a stately black woman in a long, sheaflike white dress walked over to seat us. On the stage beneath a blue light a trio played an old Miles Davis number. They sounded pretty good, too, but you had to listen above the undercurrent of conversation; the crowd had obviously come for something else.

And there was no mistaking when it came. A hushed reverence settled over the room; even the other white table, filled with leisure suits out for a good time, became uncomfortably quiet. It was hard to tell why at first. Then I realized that someone had stepped onto the back of the stage. Mitch whispered, "There he is," and made an awkward attempt at a wave. Ben Tiner was a short gray-haired man, undistinguished-looking in brown trousers and a rumpled shirt. But Mitch was right; he really did play marvelous sax. You almost knew he would from the moment he lifted the instrument out of its case; simply hefting it between his two hands seemed to demand all his attention and all his affection as well. And when he began to play, he gave you the feeling that there was nothing else in the world he would rather be doing and no one else anywhere he would rather be playing for.

He played a lot of old favorites, like "Kind of Blue" and "Night Train." And he played some other numbers I had never heard that he sounded perfectly at home with, as if he had played them thirty years ago in the cafés and bars of New York. After about forty-five minutes he walked out among the tables with his sax. He stopped in front of us and told Cassie to request any song she liked and he would play it. She asked him to play "String of Pearls," and he walked back up to the stage and bent his knees and leaned back until you thought the sax was going to topple him over. After the number was over, we stood and applauded and I thought he nodded and smiled slightly in our direction.

"Didn't you think he was marvelous?" Mitch asked.

"He was terrific," I said.

In the car driving home, Cassie said, "I had a wonderful time tonight."

"So did I."

"You didn't like the party," she corrected me.

"No, not much," I admitted, "but there was a lot that I did like."

"Life ought to be filled with things like that."

"Like what?" I asked.

"Like dancing alone by the side of a pool and sweet old men who play good jazz saxophone and —"

"And what?"

"And people you care for."

I was on the point of replying, "Maybe it is and you just don't know it," when she suddenly threw her head back and laughed. "*God*," she said. "I'm even beginning to *sound* like a debutante."

I pulled between the great stone pillars and in a self-conscious silence drove for what seemed like a half mile up the winding brick driveway toward the house. At the door she said good night almost breathlessly and disappeared inside. I stood for a moment and let my eyes wander over the shadowed stone facing of that fantastic house, and then

I tried to picture Cassie as she moved and breathed inside it. But I could not, so I walked back to my car and drove home.

The next morning two cups of coffee and a copy of the *Miami Herald* had not managed to drive Cassie from my mind. Without trying I remembered exactly how she looked when she walked down that gleaming marble staircase, and the cool moist feel of her skin when we danced alone on the concrete beside the pool, and what she had said in the car as we drove home. I thought about that for a long time. But since I am by nature skeptical, I put it — most of it, anyway — down to the party or to the moon or perhaps to the measures of some very-far-off music that had not even reached my ears, and I got ready to go to work.

I was forty-five minutes late. When I walked into the city room, McDermott looked up and peered at me over his bifocals and did not say a word. My desk was covered with work, and every time he looked toward me I managed to be shifting through papers or typing furiously. By the end of the day I had typed five paragraphs of a story on dog racing that I should have finished in three hours and had taken two obituaries.

The next day was turning into the same thing. Finally I picked up the phone and called Cassie's house. The maid answered and said she wasn't home.

"Do you know when she'll be back?"

"She don't say." She sounded strangely uncooperative and in one unlikely moment I wondered if she'd been instructed not to put me through. But I dismissed that and left my name along with the phone number, even though I knew she already had it.

When I had heard nothing by Thursday I called again; this time there was no answer at all. I called back, cradling the

phone against my ear, and let it ring through the stone corridors of that vast house while I typed out a few random lines.
After about five minutes, an unfamiliar male voice answered.

I asked to speak to Cassie.

"Miss Cassie not home."

"Who is this?" I demanded, sounding a good bit more
proprietary than I had a right to.

"This is Luther, the gardener," the voice said.

"Well, who is home?" I asked in exasperation.

"Mr. Fairchild in the library."

"Then let me speak to him."

There was a sharp noise as if the receiver had been dropped
against the granite floor, followed by several long minutes of
silence. Finally I heard the phone being picked up and then
a grunt that might have been Mr. Fairchild saying hello.

I decided that it was, identified myself, and asked if he
knew where Cassie was.

"Nope."

"Well, if you hear from her, will you ask her to call me?"

He said he would in a voice that was gruff but did not
sound exactly unfriendly.

By this time I think I was more perplexed than angry. But
I guess I was plenty angry, too. I slammed the phone down
and ripped a piece of copy out of my typewriter. McDermott
peered up at me with mild curiosity and said, "What's been
eating you, Phillips?"

That is the kind of question I never have a suitable answer
for.

five

I don't want to give the impression that Cassie occupied all my thoughts. On the contrary, for me it was turning into a busy summer. June was slipping by, and most people were beginning to think about outdoor barbecues or long weekends on the beach at Pensacola. I had other things on my mind. On the last Friday night in the month a policeman shot and killed a robbery suspect in a black housing project on the Northside. As it happened, the suspect was an unarmed seventeen-year-old girl. And since it was a very warm night — with a taste of the kind of heat we would have later that summer — a number of the residents gathered on their porches and on their back stoops to watch and to make their feelings known to the officers of the law. Soon they had come off of their porches and had spilled over into the street until there was an angry-looking crowd surrounding the two white policemen standing with their guns still drawn in the tepid night air. One of them — I believe it was a certain officer Larry Pitts, a young man with blond hair and a red pockmarked face — managed to reach the patrol car and radio for help before the crowd closed around them and took the guns out of their hands. Three minutes later a dozen squad cars had sealed off the area, and twenty minutes after that a tactical squad dressed in army fatigues and flak jackets swept through shooting out streetlights. At the sound of their M-16s and the shattering glass, most of the crowd scattered, although one group made a faint attempt to turn over a squad car. The police shoved, prodded, and pounded some of the slower members of the crowd back onto their porches and behind their screen doors. But they made few arrests and later an editorial in our paper praised the authorities "for showing restraint" at the same time that it called for "a full investigation into the unexplained death of a seventeen-year-old girl."

At any rate, we had our hands full during the entire week. The steamy air was filled with charges and countercharges, demonstrations and counterdemonstrations. Small but determined contingents from SCAR (Southerners Concerned About Racism) marched to the taunts of white-robed Klansmen who looked as if they'd crawled out of the nearest swamp, while harried police officers, sweating in their bulletproof vests, strained to hold them apart.

So, as I said, I had other things on my mind. And when the telephone rang late one afternoon and I heard her unexpected voice, it is a wonder I recognized it at all. Yet Cassie was never more clearly present to me than when I heard the sound of her voice. It was not merely that she possessed a rich vibrant quality that reminded you a little of Tallulah Bankhead (who was actually a distant cousin of Mr. Fairchild's). There was more to it than that. Sometimes when she spoke, you felt as though her voice were filled with a question that was so important she dared not ask it. And at other times it was as if she had asked the question after all, and you could hear the answer trembling in her throat — the faint but unmistakable note of disappointment.

It was this — the disappointing answer to the question —

that I heard that afternoon when she said, "Hello, Nick. How have you been?"

So I was taken aback at first. Then I remembered that I was annoyed at her. "How have *you* been?" I asked, feeling that I was due an explanation. "*Where* have you been?"

"I'm sorry. I've been busy." Now question and answer both were lost and her voice sounded simply empty and hopeless.

But I was determined not to let her off that easily. "I'll say you have. I've left messages with everyone in the house, including the gardener."

"Don't be angry with me, Nick," she said flatly. "I've been having a bad time."

"What's the matter?" I said. "Is something wrong?"

She laughed, but not as if she had found anything funny. "No, there's nothing wrong. Not a thing in the whole wide world." She did not even seem to be talking to me.

I asked again. "Where have you been?"

"Different places," she said. "I spent a few nights with a friend of Daddy's."

"Where are you now?"

Instead of answering that, she said, "Why don't you meet me tomorrow?" And before she hung up, she said, that new lost note in her voice, "I really need a friend, Nick."

I wasn't sure whether to feel flattered or disappointed at that. A little bit of both, I guess.

I waited at Delos', where Cassie was supposed to meet me for lunch, for an hour and a half. She didn't show. When I got to work, I found a note on my desk typed in McDermott's absurd personal shorthand: "gn 2 frisco - srry i mssd yu - bak n a fw dys - C." I thought that was a nice touch of McDermott's, underlining the C.

Frisco. Well that was fine, too, whatever the hell it meant.

I needed to get some work done for a change, and I was going to put the entire Fairchild clan out of my mind. That night I went out with Hurlbut and Maynard Walsh, the assistant city editor. Walsh is a middle-aged bachelor who collects World War II memorabilia, and he can give renditions of Hitler's speeches in what sounds like pretty fair German considering that he doesn't understand a word of it.

six

*T*he dead girl's name was Fonda Lyn Trafford, although three weeks went by before the police found that out. And by then the story was good for no more than a few paragraphs on the back of the supermarket section. Still, it had stayed alive longer than most murders. The reason for that was simple: as long as the girl had remained a mystery, no more than a milk-white form in the moonlight, she had aroused interest. We had even received phone calls from readers claiming to know who she was or the circumstances surrounding her death.

In the end, of course, the police discovered her identity the hard way. They traced an article of clothing — a pair of mauve nylon panties — to a small specialty shop in downtown Bessemer. Fonda Trafford, nineteen years old when she died, was from Luverne, a tiny town in the southeast corner of Alabama almost, but not quite, within spitting distance of the Gulf Coast (sometimes known as the Redneck Riviera). She had actually been born in the town of Dora, a small mining community not far from Hueytown itself. Her father had held jobs in the area — as an auto mechanic, a coal miner, a farm laborer — until the girl was about ten. After that he was called to preach, or so Harris put it to me. The family wandered for a time back and forth across central

Alabama and Mississippi; maybe Trafford thought of himself as a latter-day version of Lorenzo Dow, saving souls in the wilderness of the New South. Five years before his daughter's death he'd managed to get his own church — a small Baptist splinter sect in Luverne. Sometime after that, Harris told me, Trafford's wife had left him — or he had run her off, that wasn't quite clear. The girl stayed with the father, but relations between them soured. Finally she'd simply up and left, hadn't communicated with either parent for more than a year.

The police had been busy lately tracing Fonda Trafford's movements. She went first to Mobile, then on to New Orleans, where she stayed about six weeks. For the past ten months she'd been living near Birmingham in a trailer shared sporadically by a girlfriend. She'd held a job as a waitress, but only for a few weeks, and her boss said he didn't think anything of it when she failed to show one morning, just put the HELP WANTED sign back in the window.

"So there was nobody to go looking for her," Harris said. "Nobody missed her."

With the name, and a picture to go with it, the girl's death flared briefly back across the front page like the evanescent trail of a falling star. The picture was a worn wallet-sized photo taken against a blank gray backdrop — probably a high-school yearbook picture — that had come from the girl's mother. After all this time the photo seemed to be nothing more than a curious artifact. Just a shade overexposed, it showed a pretty, girlish face framed with dark blond hair that did not quite reach to the shoulders. She wore a black drape with a V-shaped neckline that must have come to a point right below the picture, and a gold add-a-bead necklace. If the photographer had tried to avoid any nuance of individual expression or character, he had largely succeeded. There was no hint of what lay behind the face, though there was something sensual — not high-schoolish at all — in the set of the mouth.

"She was a good girl who wouldn't cause trouble to no one. She just wanted to be her own person," the mother sobbed when she came to Birmingham to identify the body.

"The flesh is rank and ends in dust," said the father when I called him in Luverne. "It is the soul we must pray for, that it be spared the everlasting fire."

That made pretty good copy. Besides, there wasn't too much else to say. The police had no leads — at least none they were talking about — and they appealed to the public for information, listing a confidential department phone number.

I kept on drinking with Walsh and Hurlbut — either out of boredom or out of habit. A couple of weeks passed during which my life was a routine of work, late-night bars, and blear bloodshot mornings. On one of those mornings I was pulled from sleep by an insistent knocking that at first I believed — with some justification — to be inside my own head. I sat up and reached for my watch. Eight-thirty. I lay back and listened, exploring my skull with the tips of my fingers. Either someone was at the door, or else I was in much worse shape than I had imagined possible. I thought it over, wondering vaguely which of the two I would prefer. Then I turned over on my stomach and put the pillow behind my head. More knocking. Someone was at the door.

I pulled an old terrycloth robe out of the dirty clothes and lumbered through the living room. Finding someone at my doorstep at an unwelcome hour of the morning was an occupational hazard for me. It could have been a salesman or the fat handyman from the landlord's office. But in the final analysis I do not believe I was really surprised to find Cassie standing on my balcony in a spanking white tennis outfit, outlined rather splendidly against the clear blue sky. She was wearing a little yellow visor and looked for all the world like an advertisement for some summer resort.

"Hi," she said. "Isn't it beautiful out?"

The daylight seemed inhumanly bright, and my eyes wouldn't quite focus. "I wouldn't know."

Cassie had her hands on her hips, and she shifted her feet and looked at me. "Well. Can I come in or what?"

I opened the door all the way and made an elaborate gesture for her to enter.

She walked rather absently around the living room. "Do you know this is the first time I've seen your apartment." She pitched her visor onto the sofa as if she meant to stay awhile.

"It's not at its best in the morning." I was looking at the remains of yesterday's breakfast in the sink. "Do you want some coffee?"

"Mmmm," she said, "maybe, if you're having some."

I filled the kettle, then turned my attention to measuring the beans out exactly and grinding them up. Cassie was standing beside the kitchen table, drumming lightly on it with the tips of her fingers.

"Do you want toast, too?" Without looking at her or waiting for an answer, I reached for the whole wheat in the back of the cabinet and pulled with such force that a couple of cans of soup came spilling out with it. When I bent down to pick them up, I felt her hand on the sleeve of my robe.

"Don't sulk," she said. "I couldn't help it. I just had to get the hell out of Dodge for a few days."

"That's your business," I said, although it came out sounding much colder than I had intended. To soften it I added, "Did you have to go all the way to the West Coast?"

She looked at me for a minute without comprehending, then burst into a fit of laughter.

"What's funny?" I demanded.

"You are," she said. "Frisco's three hours south of here

and has a population of about a hundred and ten. God, it's a good thing I didn't go to Athens, Alabama, or Paris, Tennessee; you'd probably have given me up for dead."

I frowned, perhaps to keep from looking as sheepish as I felt. "What made you go there?"

"It didn't matter, it could have been anywhere. When I left here I just wanted to find a hole to crawl into, someplace where no one could crawl in after me."

"That sounds lovely. What did you do for fun?"

"Read some," she answered, ignoring the sarcasm, "walked in the woods mostly. It's marvelous down there, full of hemlock and wild magnolia."

"Did anyone else know where you were?"

"I left a note for Melissa so she wouldn't worry."

"Who's Melissa?"

"Melissa Hollingsworth," she said. "A friend of Daddy's. She puts me up sometimes when I can't take it up there anymore." She was pacing in my living room, and she began rubbing the sides of her bare arms as if she were chilled.

I asked if she wanted a sweater, but she shook her head no.

"You don't know me very well, I mean *really* know me, do you, Nick?"

I said, "Sometimes I think I do," but she ignored that and went on.

"And you don't know much about my family either."

I listened.

"Did you know Daddy was an alcoholic? Did you know I used to come home from school and find him passed out on the library floor. And after the doctors told him his ulcers were killing him, the joke among my friends was that he had taken to giving himself bourbon enemas. It might have been true, for all I know."

"He doesn't look like an alcoholic," I said.

"No," she said. "He's not drinking anymore. He saved himself from *that* particular form of suicide a few years back. And then there's my precious brother," she went on, "Mama's pride and joy. He never touches liquor; she's managed to turn him against that just like she's turned him against everything that has anything to do with Daddy. No, he's not an alcoholic; Mother can be proud of that." And she gave a small grim smile. "He's a junkie." I must have looked surprised, because she said, "Oh, I know all this sounds like a cheap script, but it's true. I've seen him during parties at the club disappear onto the golf course, then float back in, his face glowing and his eyes glazed over like windowpanes."

I was beginning to believe her. But she was right, it did resemble a bad movie, and I had the feeling of watching a good actress who was wasted in it.

She shivered again and clasped her arms. "Sometimes I feel as if something horrible is going to happen to us." I was still thinking over this last statement when she began walking up and down the room once more and broke into a monologue.

Cassie talked about her father more than anyone else. "Daddy and I are very close," she told me. "When I was younger, we were always going off together. It really bugged Mother.

"I remember once when I was in college the whole bloody family got together in New York for Mother's birthday. We were at '21,' I think, somewhere really expensive and tacky like that. Mother said it was her favorite restaurant; of course it was probably the first time in her life she'd ever set foot in the place. Anyway, after we'd been there for four hours and after Mother had been bowed and scraped to by everyone in uniform, Daddy and I managed to slip away. We said we were going back to the hotel, but we went to the Museum of Modern Art and browsed around — both of us like Matisse best. Mother managed to find us somehow: She caught up with us in the sculpture garden. I remember we were standing right in front of one of those Calder mobiles when I heard this woman screaming. At first I didn't know who she was, just one of those lunatics you're always running into in New York.

"Then I saw it was Mother. She stood in the middle of the garden shouting at us, at Daddy mostly. She said he had deserted her and the baby — Timmy was seventeen years old at the time — anyway, she said he had deserted them in the middle of a strange unfriendly city. She said they might have been mugged or kidnapped for all he cared, and she said she'd have his ass for it. Mother always was a good talker. Everyone in the place just stared. I remember one woman in a full-length black mink coat, and two middle-aged men in identical blue blazers — fags probably — who positively cringed. And Mother standing there like a madwoman ranting in that south-Georgia accent." Cassie's mother was from Macon. "Ugh," she said as if the memory of that accent were suddenly too much for her.

"Daddy never said a word. He just stood as calm as you please and looked past her as if she were another of the statues. That made her a whole lot angrier of course. I pretended I didn't know her and went on walking through the garden looking at sculptures. Then I went into the cafeteria and sat down and had a glass of wine, and I could still hear her screaming from inside. I don't remember exactly what happened after that, but I know Daddy had hell to pay when they got back home."

She stopped. She was standing in front of the living-room window with her back to me; the sun slanting in through the closed blinds made pencil streaks of yellow light across her bare legs. "You know," she said slowly, "sometimes I think the real reason I hate Mother is that I'm afraid one day I'm going to be like her." She shook her head. "Oh, I don't know what I'm talking about." Then she turned and laughed abruptly, and her voice dropped a full octave. "Listen," she said. "Don't pay any attention to me. I'm just talking. I shouldn't be going on like this."

I was pouring the coffee, but I kept watching her. "You were right in what you said a few minutes ago," I told her.

She looked puzzled. "When?"

"You said I don't know you very well. But that's only the half of it. You don't really know me either. We've never, either of us, taken the trouble to get to know one another."

Cassie frowned for a moment, but only for a moment. "I wouldn't want to hurt you, Nick," she said, again in that quiet brooding voice.

That reminded me that I was still a little angry. "Fine," I said, "we're agreed on that."

She ignored whatever annoyance was in my voice. "What do you do if you want to get to know someone? We could tell each other things no one else knows." She stopped and laughed. "Well, I've already told you all the family secrets, and look where it got us.

"I know," she said. "Why don't you take me out on a date, a real date. We could pretend we were courting."

I laughed, not altogether in amusement. "*Are* we courting?"

"I mean it," she insisted. "Where do people go in this town when they're on a date?"

"The backseat of a car," I suggested.

"Don't be vulgar," she said. "They go dancing, or" — perhaps remembering the debut party — "they go to the movies. Of course, that's what people do."

I believed she was really serious. "I have to work every night this week," I said. "Except Saturday."

"All right. Saturday, then."

seven

Saturday night was cool and clear — as cool and clear as it ever gets down here in mid-July. There were a few stars visible beyond the city's neon haze. A light mist around the moon lent it a soft translucent quality, as if it were cut from a fine piece of cloth. Cassie had been staying at Melissa Hollingsworth's, out near the Shady Vale Country Club, for most of the week. I pulled into the concrete driveway, got out, and walked around to the garage apartment. Before I knocked, Cassie opened the door.

She was wearing a straight khaki-colored skirt and pale peach blouse that buttoned up the front. And penny loafers. It was the sort of schoolgirl look that was just beginning to appear in Bloomingdale's ads in the Sunday *Times* and has never gone out of fashion at some southern universities. I held the car door open, and she let the fingers of one hand rest lightly on my arm as she stepped in. While I backed out of the driveway, she said, "I hope I wasn't too forward the other day."

"What do you mean?"

"You know, when I practically asked you out."

At first I was puzzled, and I wondered if she was having some sort of private joke. Gradually the truth dawned on me. All this was her way of trying to put our date on what she considered its proper footing. I glanced sideways at her. Whatever we had now become was summed up by Cassie sitting perfectly straight against the seat, her shoulders primly squared, hands folded away in her lap.

We were on our way to the Alabama Theater. Most of the moviehouses downtown, the ones that hadn't closed down, served up X-rated schoolgirls and kung fu killers. But the Alabama had tried to survive by becoming an "art house." Built in the twenties in the style of a Moorish palace, it was too imposing for the soft-core porno audience. This week a Bogart festival was playing.

The movie was one of those Bogart made after *Casablanca*. He plays the usual sort of character, hard as gun metal on the outside, but deep down a man of principle, an idealist, and a soft touch for anyone who finds him out. There is a woman involved. She is beautiful and speaks with an exotic accent and at first, for no discernible reason except perhaps that she misunderstands him, treats Bogart with coldness and contempt. Later she has a change of heart and throws herself at him. In the end, of course, Bogart is left alone. But it is gratifying to behold him up there, alone and alive. And it is gratifying, too, to see the Nazis or the Fascists or whoever they are, beaten back by his cunning and his courage.

So I left the theater with a good feeling. And it felt good to step into the uncertain territory of the late-night streets with Cassie on my arm in her crisp khaki skirt and peach-colored blouse.

In the car she leaned over and put an arm on my shoulder and asked, "Where shall we go from here?"

We drove up a narrow one-lane road that winds along the rim of the mountain to a secluded spot I remembered from years ago. It was deserted now except for the statue of Vulcan, a little farther up the mountain, looming high above us with his wrought-iron gaze.

"I'll bet you came up here when you were younger," Cassie said.

"Maybe once or twice."

"Who with?"

I thought about it. "Well, there was a cheerleader named Linda Lankford."

"Linda Lankford," she exclaimed. "My God, I haven't thought about her in years." Cassie gave me a rather appraising look. "So you like big boobs."

"I was impressionable."

"She was sort of *obvious*. I wonder whatever happens to girls like that."

"They get married, they get divorced, they get drunk — not necessarily in that order."

"I don't believe that," she said. "I mean, it may be true about Linda, but it's not true for you."

"What does that mean?"

"It means that's not really the way you look at things — cynically. That's all right for McDermott or some of those other hacks you've told me about. But it isn't what you're really like."

"I see." I considered that. "And I suppose you're going to tell me what I am really like."

"That's easy. You're a romantic. I knew that the first day I saw you."

I was going to protest, but I saw it wouldn't get me anywhere. Instead I leaned toward Cassie and we kissed, our lips meeting a few inches in front of the rearview mirror. To be with a girl in the front seat of a Chevrolet is to be reminded of the sheer physical awkwardness of lovemaking; the human body is not precisely shaped for it, even in the best of circumstances. So it was the pure practical necessity, as much as anything else, that led me to whisper to Cassie, "Do you want to come home with me?"

In answer she murmured something I didn't exactly understand, but the sound of her voice was such a pleasurable sensation against my ear that it sent agreeable shivers up and down my spine. I turned around, backing the car as far onto the shoulder as I dared, and headed down the mountain.

We were quiet, very quiet, all the way home. All I heard was the muffled drumming of the Chevrolet engine and, at times, a slight ringing in my ears.

When we walked into my apartment, Cassie looked around as if she hadn't seen the place before. "This is nice," she said. "I like the rug."

It was an Oriental, much faded, that had belonged to my grandmother. I looked at its tree-of-life design as if I had never laid eyes on it. "Needs to be cleaned," I said.

She said, "Oh."

I asked if I could get her a drink, but she didn't want one. I did. Then I remembered there was nothing in the house except a bottle of pale, dry sherry.

"Sit down," I said, motioning toward the couch. It was an overstuffed modern sofa that I had bought on some misguided impulse and was impossible to sit upon. We ended up in a semi-sprawl with our heads lolling beside one another across the sofa back, looking up at the ceiling.

"Jesus," Cassie said, "I'm as nervous as a virgin before the 4-H Club dance."

I leaned over, supporting my weight with one hand on the spongy sofa cushion, and kissed her. She put a hand to the side of my cheek. "I want to go to bed," she said.

I stood and helped her to her feet. This time I could hear my heart beating, except that it was no longer in my chest, it was somewhere far back inside my throat. We walked together a little stiffly into my bedroom, like a couple walking out onto a dance floor for the very first time. Cassie turned to face me and began unbuttoning her top. I put my hands on her shoulders, and she arched her arms behind her while I slipped the blouse off down to her wrists. She bent over backward a little, and I kissed her. Out of the corner of my eye I watched the blouse drop to the floor, billowing like a kite on its way down. I had one hand on the back of her waist, and I was seized with the sudden unreasoning conviction that we were about to topple over backward. But we stood our ground and it subsided, although I kept my hand around her. With my other hand I unfastened the front of her bra. The clasp fell away, revealing fine bare skin, the cups of the bra still covering her widely spaced breasts.

She reached up and with a quick careless movement swept the straps off her shoulders. Perhaps because of the light, her breasts looked an almost apricot color, the nipples darkly pink and erect. She lifted my hand and put it over her. I moved my other hand along the waistband of her skirt. She stopped it, and for one heart-wrenching second I thought I had misunderstood. But she said, "You next," and unbuttoned my shirt.

There was no clasp to her skirt, nothing but a flimsy elastic band. She put her hands to her waist, one a little lower than the other, slid them down and rotated her hips in a sort of bump and grind, only it was more girlish and more practical than that. The skirt slipped below her waist, caught for a mere instant where her legs bowed outward a little, and dropped to her feet.

I stepped back. Cassie was standing with the doorway behind her, and the light from the living room gathered along the edges of her bare skin, around the points of her hair. I put my hands on her waist, moving them up her sides, then all the way back down until my fingertips felt the cool smooth curving outward of her buttocks. She took one of my hands and moved it slowly around and pressed it to the front of her. My heartbeat wasn't in my throat anymore; it was racing down my legs, echoing among the myriad bones of my skull, bursting somewhere far inside of me. Then Cassie whispered, "Wait." She stepped quickly on her toes into the living room, reached something out of her purse, then disappeared into the bathroom. I was surprised at the small, perfectly human dimensions of her body as she walked through my apartment.

I sat on the edge of the bed and my excitement subsided a little, although that was just as well, for I was plenty excited enough. A million things were crowding like a fever through my brain. I thought of everything Cassie had told me, all that I knew about her and all that I would probably never know. I thought that making love for the first time when it is someone you really care for is uncertain territory, possibly filled with danger, and it demands all of your skill and all of your cunning. And then before I could think about how absurd that sounded, Cassie reappeared and stretched herself across me on the bed, arms stiffly straddling my chest. I looked up and met her face; she wore a quizzical, half-amused expression that seemed to comprehend a part at least of what I had been thinking, and to pardon it.

We made love. Even now, making love with Cassie is not something I can clearly describe. It seemed a fluid and involuntary action that enveloped my brain as much as my body.

Yet even our most exhilarating moments were often perplexing and oddly unsatisfying. At times Cassie was filled with a sort of recklessness, a desperate intensity that seemed to leave me behind. And the more I reached after her, the more inaccessible she became, walled off within the fierce lonely pleasure of her lovemaking. Her remoteness only made me want her that much more, and I tried with a recklessness of my own to break through the wall and to reach her.

eight

*U*sually we saw each other at my place or in the little garage apartment Cassie sometimes occupied at Melissa Hollingsworth's. Even though we were together often, I had the continual sense that I was just getting to know her. Sometimes she would suddenly open up, like a rose that overwhelms you with its wholeness and elaborate perfection. At other times she withdrew and getting through to her was a little like peeling away layers from an onion, and just as unpleasant and as meagerly rewarding.

Most of the time Melissa left us alone. But I had the vague feeling that she approved. As if to confirm this, Melissa called one evening at my apartment and asked me to meet her. She said she wanted to talk. About what? I wondered.

"Shall I drive up to the house?" I asked.

"Oh, no," she said quickly. "Let's not bother Cassie with this. I have to go to Highlands to work on a set. Why don't you meet me about nine o'clock, love."

I said I'd be there.

Highlands was no more than a mile from where I lived. It had originally been built by a fraternal order as a country retreat in the middle of a meadow overlooking a small lake on the outskirts of town. By the 1900s it had become The

53

Country Club of Birmingham, and the meadow was a golf course, the lake a water hazard. Later, after the country club retreated over the mountain to Shady Vale, the place stood empty, golf course reverted back to meadow. Local preservationists said the building, a confusion of Victorian gables and soaring Georgian columns, was a historical landmark. And so it was, I suppose, in a city that measures its history in ten-year intervals. At last the city restored it as a recreation center, with the golf course open to the public and a private tennis club preserving a little of the old aura of rank and status.

I had played tennis there once or twice since returning to Birmingham. The marble-floored lobby, formerly the grand ballroom, was a true melting pot. There were the sporting rednecks, a bit paunchy in bright knit shirts and Expanda-waist slacks, cradling their putters in the crooks of their arms as if carrying shotguns. A few black foursomes. And of course the tennis "bums" from over the mountain, who just had time for one set before meeting a client or going home to drink the rest of the afternoon away. All of them rubbed loins in the lobby and shared the same watercooler, while from three shadowy corners of the terra-cotta ceiling winged cupids smiled doubtfully down upon them. The cupid who had occupied the fourth corner must have been a casualty long ago.

I had never been to Highlands at night before. The long driveway wound up through the golf course past humpbacked greens that seemed to ride the hills like sinister animals. Three cars were parked in front of the clubhouse, but they appeared abandoned in the big vacant lot. The building itself loomed like a great shut-up old house. The odd-angled gables cast their shadows every which way in the moonlight, and the front columns shone a luminous white.

Inside, emptied of the redneck golfers and tennis bums, it looked like a completely different place. The lobby was an expanse of white marble floor, larger and more remote, untouchable. Hanging from the ceiling were cheap fluorescent fixtures that obviously didn't belong, and the hall simply refused to light up for them. The cupids stood back in their corners, shadowy and mysterious. I felt like an intruder. I imagined that it might have looked something like this if I had walked in seventy-five years ago as the lights were dimming after the last dance. A balcony encircled the room, and at the far end it was broken by a long staircase that descended slowly out onto the dance floor. That was the only movement in the room — all else was watching and waiting.

"Over here, love." At the sound, the first I had heard inside the place, I started. Melissa stood in a doorway beneath the balcony. Barefoot, wearing paint-stained jeans and a sweatshirt, and holding a paintbrush, she looked a little like a hippie who had wandered in out of an earlier decade. But her age, somewhere near forty, showed clearly in her face and in her gray-streaked hair.

"Come on," she said, "there's work to be done."

She led me into a storeroom off the lobby where paints and newspapers and stretches of canvas were scattered across the floor. Several people were working intently. One was a young man who must have been six foot six and weighed at least three hundred pounds. He was introduced to me as Avon, and he was the most effeminate large man I have ever seen. He walked on tiny mincing feet and had small delicate hands. There was also a frail blond woman named Sylvie who spoke with a lisp. They were working on a set for a local production of *A Midsummer Night's Dream*. The play opened in two weeks, and Melissa seemed to regard this as if it were a national emergency. Whatever she had called me to discuss seemed forgotten. As far as she was concerned, I had come out to work on the set; and since Sylvie and the fat young man assumed the same thing, I reluctantly accepted a paintbrush. I worked at a backdrop filling in leaves on great unearthly-looking trees — the forest of Puck and Oberon and Titania. It was a warm night and before I had finished, my face was smudged with dark metallic green and blue where I had wiped away sweat.

Around eleven Sylvie started getting ready to leave, and Melissa told Avon to go, too, that I would help lock up.

When we were alone she said, "I'm glad you came up here tonight," as if I had been carried there by some random impulse instead of her phone call. "I've been wanting to talk to you."

"What about?" I asked as casually as I could.

"I'm not sure what you know about me, Nick, or how much you've heard."

All I knew about Melissa was what I had pieced together from Cassie. The daughter of a self-made millionaire who had begun as a sewage subcontractor and ended up as a big-time developer, Melissa had married one of her father's construction foremen. The marriage wasn't much of a success and they had lived on her money or her father's name until they parted amicably a few years back.

"I'd like you to think well of me," Melissa continued insistently. "That's partly why I'm telling you this. You know that Cassie's father and I are friends. Actually I've known him for years — Birmingham is such a small town in that way — but it's only lately, in a way through Cassie, that we've become close. After her breakdown, after she got back from —," she hesitated delicately — "from up east, he suggested she move in with me. I'd only been divorced for a year and a half, and I liked the idea of someone nearby. I know it's been good for me; Cassie can be the best company in the world — she could charm the skin off a snake if she wanted to. I think it's been good for her too, don't you?"

I was both flattered and annoyed by this appeal to me as

an authority on Cassie's state of mind. I gave what I thought was a noncommittal nod of the head.

After a moment she asked, "What do you think of Chapell?" using for the first time the name Mr. Fairchild was called by.

"He's a difficult person to know," I said. "Besides, I've only spoken to him a couple of times."

"Well, he likes you," Melissa told me. "I think he's a little relieved Cassie's taken up with you. Dear God," she burst out laughing, "you should have seen her last boyfriend. He called himself a sculptor. But the only things I ever saw him do looked like they were made out of Silly Putty. 'Pure plasticity,' he called them."

I did not particularly care to be reminded of Cassie's former lover, even if the joke was at his expense. So I was relieved, for the moment at least, when she turned the conversation back to Mr. Fairchild. "I guess you know Chapell and I see each other pretty frequently."

I guessed that I knew it, too, whenever I chose to think about it.

"We have an unusual relationship," she went on, "one that most people couldn't understand. They say we're having an affair, but you know how this town likes to talk. Half the women in Shady Vale run their mouths like an outdoor toilet."

I waited for her to explain just what sort of an unusual relationship it was. When she didn't, I asked, "Is there any truth to what they say?" It wasn't exactly a tactful question, but I had decided that since she chose to put me squarely into this mess, I had a right to ask it.

But Melissa didn't answer. She reminded me of Cassie; neither of them ever answered a question directly. In fact I wasn't even sure she'd heard it. She was gazing beyond me out into the old ballroom, as if she were watching a single pair of lovers perform their elaborately patterned dance.

"How much do you know about Chapell?" she asked, still looking off into the distance.

"Not much," I said. "Just one or two things Cassie's told me."

"He's a very sensitive person. And he hasn't been exactly blessed in the state of matrimony." She gave a short explosive laugh. "I don't mean to be catty, but Julia" — Cassie's mother — "could make Madame Defarge look like Saint Theresa on Sunday."

Then she became almost solemn. "It's just such a waste, Nick. He deserves better than this. And I don't think you could blame him for anything he might do, either," she said defiantly, as if she were daring me to pronounce some sort of judgment.

But I had no desire to pronounce judgment on anyone, nor, I thought grimly to myself, to pronounce absolution either. And I was getting a little tired of hearing confessions. And so, partly because I hoped it would discourage her from telling me any more, I asked what I had been brought up to believe was the rudest question you could put to anyone: "How did he make all his money?"

But it seemed to be just the question she was waiting for. "He inherited it, love. From his mother. She was a Chapell," Melissa said, as if that ought to explain everything. And it did explain a good deal. You couldn't live in Birmingham without having at least heard of the Chapells. In the years after the Civil War, when most southern families were lucky if they could still remember where the silver was buried, the Chapells had had the single-mindedness to build an empire, of which Birmingham was the center. The Alabama Coal and Iron Company had started off producing cannonballs for the Confederate navy; but the Chapells built it up into one of the largest holders of ore mines and furnaces in the country — until J. P. Morgan took it off their hands. Now all they owned were a few thousand acres of real estate and a couple of banks.

"Old Mr. Fairchild was pretty well fixed, too," Melissa said. "Before he was through, his law firm was doing the work for his wife's family, and for others like them. Chapell didn't want any part of that." I remembered now that Cassie had told me her father had quit law school to study architecture, to have a fling at reformist politics, to write poetry even. Her grandfather had been so enraged he disinherited him.

"Everything Chapell has came through his mother," Melissa went on, "and I don't mean just money. He was named for her family. He was her only child — she died of childbed fever three days after he was born. After that his father was so grief-stricken he wouldn't have the baby in the house. Chapell was raised by his mother's elder sister, an eccentric spinster who had been a Chinese missionary. He didn't see his father again until he was ten years old. By then Mr. Fairchild had remarried; I think he must have picked the tackiest woman he could find. She was a salesgirl, and she never let Chapell's mother's name be mentioned in that house, not even years later, after his father died. Why, he doesn't have a picture of her, doesn't even know for certain what she looked like. She was supposed to have been a great beauty and terribly headstrong. She ran off with his father — old Mr. Fairchild came from good Mississippi stock but he wasn't in the Chapells' league. The family tried to buy him off."

"What was his mother's name?" I asked.

"Cassandra," she said. "Cassandra Chapell."

"Cassandra," I repeated, and the sound seemed to echo through the room. "So that's where Cassie comes by it."

She said, "The name you mean?" but I thought she knew I meant a good deal more than that.

Melissa shrugged. "The real irony is that Cassie's mother

is so much like her father's stepmother. Well," she added glumly, "I guess she must have been pretty once or something."

I watched for a couple of minutes while Melissa fidgeted with one of the canvas backdrops. Then I asked, "Does Mr. Fairchild — does Chapell — know you're telling me all this?"

"I didn't announce it to him, love, but I wouldn't be surprised if he knew. I thought it was time you found out how things were."

"I see."

"There's one more thing," she said. And if it was possible for Melissa to look embarrassed, she looked it now. "Occasionally Cassie can act . . . peculiar. I know she resents terribly what her mother has done to her father. I've heard her say things about Julia that I wouldn't repeat aloud, even in an empty room. Still, sometimes —"

She stopped, but I knew exactly what she meant. I had heard Cassie speak of her mother in the most cold-blooded terms imaginable, as if her odiousness were simply a quality she found amusing. Then she would quickly add, "Of course, she's my mother and I still love her." And something about that profession of love was more chilling to me than the horrid things that had come before.

"Cassie is a difficult person to understand; she's like her father in that, too," Melissa went on. "She puts up a good front and we forget what she's been through in the past year and a half. Sometimes if I mention her father, she just stares at me. You know that brooding look she has?"

I nodded. "Maybe she sees you as a threat; maybe she's afraid her parents won't stay together."

Melissa fairly hooted at this. "I can't figure out how they managed to stay together in the same room long enough to produce two children. But Cassie is a good actress — she has that Chapell histrionic streak — and once in a while she takes it into her head to play the poor little rich girl whose happy home is falling apart. Still," she admitted after a pause, "she does worry me a little sometimes."

"In what way?"

"I'm afraid she might do something to — injure herself . . . or someone close to her."

"Then why do you let her stay with you?" I asked, a note of impatience rising in my voice.

"Because I love Cassie," she answered, as if she were surprised I'd asked the question. "And I can't send her back to Black Stone Manor" — Melissa's name for the Fairchild house — "or I would feel like a monster. Besides," she added, "I promised her father I'd look out for her."

Melissa looked suddenly shy, as if she had told me a good deal more than she had intended. We sat for a few minutes without saying anything. I was thinking about the young woman Cassie was named for and about the lives she never even knew she had set in motion, and I wondered if Melissa was thinking of the same thing. It was almost oppressively quiet, and the room seemed dimmer than when I had first entered. Through the doorway I noticed for the first time the spectral glow of the fluorescent lights hanging from the ballroom ceiling. I felt once more as if I were intruding, as if we both were intruding.

The silence made me uncomfortable, and to have something to say, I asked Melissa if she often worked here late at night.

"I didn't used to. My husband said it was too dangerous. Lord knows," she said, "he would have preferred me at home doing needlepoint, or stretched out in a ladylike swoon. I like it up here. Although it gets a little lonely sometimes, and it can be as quiet as your great-aunt Sadie's grave."

I laughed. "I wouldn't be surprised if someone told me the place was haunted."

"It is," she replied.

I thought at first she was joking. "How do you know?"

"Why I've seen her, love, of course," she said, as if it were the plainest thing imaginable.

I just looked blankly at her. "Seen who?"

"A young girl in a long white dress," she said, "in there" — pointing toward the ballroom — "standing alone at the foot of the stairs."

Involuntarily I turned my head in that direction; all I could see was the empty floor stretching away through the doorway. "Come on, Melissa," I said. "You can't expect me to believe something like that."

"Well, she's there all the same," she answered calmly. "She always appears in the same place, one hand resting on the banister and one foot in front of the other on the bottom step, as if she were about to walk out onto the dance floor."

I didn't know what to say to that. Finally I asked, "What does this girl look like?"

"It's hard to see her face. You know that staircase is way back in the shadows." I gave her a wry look as if to suggest that ghosts, in my experience, were not normally obscured by shadows, but Melissa didn't pay it any attention. "She has dark hair," she went on, "and there's something lovely about her — an innocence one scarcely sees anymore. You'd like her," she told me.

I grunted at that. "Just who is she supposed to be?" I asked. "What is she —" I stopped, but Melissa looked expectantly at me. "What do you think she's doing there?"

She considered that for a moment. "I don't know who she is, but she looks like she belongs there." She wrinkled up her forehead as if she were mulling over something. "I feel sort of sorry for her. You know, I bet she's *lonely*; I bet *that's* what she is."

"And I suppose you're the only one who's seen her."

"Of course not, love, lots of people have. Avon nearly jumped out of his skin the first time."

She turned back to her canvas as casually as though she'd been gossiping about an old schoolmate. I sat thinking over what Melissa had said. A girl in a white dress. At the foot of the stairs. What the hell, I'd heard stranger stories than that from Hurlbut. And if a girl like that belonged anywhere, she certainly belonged here. Before I knew it, I found myself wondering what she might look like. I imagined that she would stand with a slight smile on her face to hide her nervousness, her head raised, gazing toward one of the cupids set in the ceiling.

For the second time that evening I started when Melissa called my name. "It's late," she said, "we'd better pack up and go home."

My watch showed nearly half past eleven. It must have taken another forty-five minutes to clean up and put everything away. The canvases had to be stretched and laid out very carefully. Some of the supplies we loaded into the back of Melissa's car. As I crossed the lobby, carrying the last two half-empty cans of paint, she called from the front porch, "Don't turn out the lights; the police say they help keep down vandalism."

I turned to take one last look around. And all at once my sense of being an intruder was so powerful that it overwhelmed me. This time it was almost palpable; it seemed to coalesce at a single spot. I stood perfectly still, balancing dizzily on the edge of a cliff. Nothing, not time or air, moved in the room. I was holding my breath, and I could feel the hairs on the back of my neck. Slowly, carefully, I turned to my right and faced the staircase at the far end of the room. It was empty. No one was there. My legs steadied beneath me, and I breathed with something like relief. And yet I felt deeply, profoundly disappointed. For a few seconds I stared at the empty staircase, and I felt an emptiness in myself that seemed to correspond to it. I do not know how to explain it, but at that precise instant I was overwhelmed with a sense of loss, of want, as if I had remembered something I did not know I had forgotten; and it was so piercing it nearly moved me to tears.

Then I turned and, through the open doorway, saw Melissa waiting for me on the front porch. She didn't see me; she was looking across the parking lot in the other direction. I shivered from head to toe. Without looking back, I walked outside.

Melissa turned around and said, "I thought you were lost, love." She looked at me curiously, but didn't ask any questions. We finished loading her car and locked up.

She put her hand on my arm and pointed up the crest of the mountain. "If you look carefully, you can see Black Stone Manor from here." I looked where she was pointing and made out the indistinct shadow of a house rising above the mountain, standing out darker than the night sky behind it. "How do you know that's the right house?"

"Because it's the biggest one up there," she said.

I shivered again, even though it was warm outside. Then I said good night, got into my car, and drove home.

The next morning I slept late. While I had coffee, I thought over what Melissa had told me. By daylight it all seemed a little bit fantastic — not just the part about the girl in the white dress — and I wasn't sure how much of any of it to believe. Nevertheless, at lunch with Cassie later that day, I brought up a couple of things I had heard, as casually as I could — that is, if there is anything casual about mentioning a ghost.

Cassie didn't bat an eye. She just said, "So you think you've seen her, too?"

"No." I said. "Melissa told me about her. Who else saw her?" I asked curiously.

"God, I don't know," she answered, as if she wasn't really interested. "I guess some of those fruitcakes Melissa works with. And Daddy claims he saw her once." She hesitated. "He told me he liked to think his mother had looked like that; she must have danced there when she was a girl and she couldn't have been much older when she died."

"I know," I said. "Melissa told me the story."

She didn't say anything, but I thought she gave me a rather odd look.

Still, I couldn't help asking, "Do you think your grandmother really looked like that?"

"Like what?"

"You know," I paused. "Like the girl in the white dress."

"I haven't the faintest idea," Cassie replied coolly. "I've never laid eyes on either of them. Besides, I don't believe in ghosts."

After that she wouldn't talk about it anymore. And later, as I drove to work beneath the relentless glare of the afternoon sun, I put it out of my mind.

nine

*F*or most of August the big story was the heat. Just turning
the pages of a newspaper was enough to make the sweat
creep out from between your fingers, while you looked at
pictures of leathery tobacco-stained farmers standing in the
middle of parched fields. Even the dogs for whom the season
is named had the good sense not to stir from that one cool
spot of earth beneath the back porch. And the bulletin board
in front of the Mount Zion Methodist Church said that on
Sunday they were going to pray for a cool breeze. It is the
same almost every year. In Alabama the August heat is an
act of God, killing more people than floods and hurricanes
combined, perhaps temporarily boosting the hopes of those
die-hard Baptists who each year expect the world to end in
fire.

There was of course nothing so dramatic — not in my life,
at least. Cassie and I saw each other often. At times she
would become absent or withdrawn, and I didn't seem able
to do much about it, and on occasion I didn't feel like trying.
Melissa told me Cassie was moody around her as well, and
I put it down to the weather. Perhaps it was simply too hot
to want to do anything except sit in front of an air conditioner
with a cool drink nearby. And wait for the heat to break, as
it always did. That is the one redeeming aspect of this sea-

son — it prickles our expectations as it prickles our skins. And so we sit and wait and hope.

Did I know what I was waiting for? Perhaps not. And if I did, I would have scarcely whispered it even to myself. Out loud I hoped for a Saturday off, or a good news story. But there was no news breaking except the heat wave itself — final tally, fourteen dead in one month, mostly old people dying shut up in silent solitary rooms.

When a story finally did come along, it was an old one that I would just as soon have forgotten. One morning in late August — a few days after the heat wave ended — McDermott called me at home. "We hear they're close to an arrest in the Trafford murder. It's your story, see what you can find out."

I had forgotten to roll my windows down, and it was about ninety degrees inside my car. While I drove through town, I tried to recall exactly what the girl's picture had looked like. All I remembered was the broken V of the black drape and the not-quite-symmetrical set of her mouth. The brown army blanket I could see much more clearly, and the plaster-of-paris leg splayed out in the beam of the headlight.

The nearest parking place was three blocks away, in front of the Greyhound bus terminal. Nashville, Louisville, and points north, eighteen hours to Cincinnati, four rest stops included. A large black woman, who for some inexplicable reason had a navy coat draped over her shoulders, was guiding two children and an oversized suitcase through the front doors. The children were clinging to the woman and giggling and swinging on the doors all at the same time. I heard the woman say, "Be still. You want me to whup your ass clear to Detroit?" Outside the terminal were three white men, two leaning against the building and the third standing with the shakes in the middle of the sidewalk. The one with the shakes stepped toward me. I thought he was going to ask for money, but he just gave me a squirrel-eyed look and stood his ground as I passed. Behind me one of the men spat onto the sidewalk. They weren't going anywhere.

By the time I stepped into the air-conditioned lobby of City Hall, I had taken off my jacket and loosened my tie, but my whole body still felt clammy with sweat. There was no one in the detectives' room except the radio dispatcher behind the desk, and she wasn't likely to tell me anything. I sat down and waited. After forty-five minutes Det. Newburn walked in. It would be Newburn. He was tall, with sideburns, and he liked to squint in a way that sometimes made him look a little like Johnny Cash. He didn't particularly care for reporters. But I knew he was investigating the Trafford case and I said, "Hello." He stared for about half a second before he recognized me. Newburn had told Mike Stankey once that I was a wise-ass and that I had made him sound like he didn't know what he was talking about, and Stankey had said, well, he wouldn't get much of an argument about that.

"I hear you're about to make an arrest."

"This is the police department," he said. "We make arrests every day." He sat down at his desk and spent five minutes shuffling through some papers. Then he turned to me again. "Ask the boss if you're interested."

At that moment Harris walked in blowing delicately on a cup of steaming coffee. He was all business; he looked at me as if he didn't know who I was.

"I understand you're ready to arrest someone for the Trafford murder," I said to him.

He frowned. "We have a suspec'," he said in an official tone of voice. "We have a suspec'."

Newburn surprised both of us by jumping in at that point. "Suspect, hell," he complained. "We got him dead to rights. One, he knew the girl. Two, we know he knew where she lived because he'd been run off once." He counted on his fingers. "Three, he was hanging around the restaurant that night. Four, he was up for rape in Mobile County three years ago, only they couldn't make it stick."

"And five," Harris said, "we just ain't got jackshit for evi-dence."

"Have you talked to him?"

"Naw," Newburn said sarcastically. "We never thought to ask him."

"Shit," said Harris, "we been talking to him since yesterday afternoon. I don't know," he sighed. "He don't have much of a story."

"What is it?"

"He says he was home all by himself drinking beer and watching TV." Harris shook his head in disgust. "I'da been more inclined to believe him if he'd told me he was jerking off."

"Where is he now?"

"Downstairs in the lockup."

"How about letting me see him," I said. "Maybe he'd tell me something he wouldn't tell you."

Harris gave me a long hard stare. Finally he let out a soft whistle through his teeth and said, "I got no objections if he don't."

The police department occupies the ground floor of City Hall; the jail is in the basement. I was led through a double set of steel doors, down a hallway, past the holding cells, and into an interrogation room barely large enough to hold a square table and three straight chairs. In the middle of the table sat an empty coffee can.

Harris's suspect — Dewitt Franklin was his name — was sitting in the corner, his shoulders hunched forward, looking toward the floor. He wore gray pants and a tan shirt, and the heels of his feet protruded from the white cotton jail slippers. He did not raise his head until the door was closed, and then

I saw that his eyes were the color of wet cement. After I had stood there for thirty seconds, I felt like I had been looking at him all my life. He could have been the fellow who cleaned your windshield at the gas station back when they still cleaned your windshield at the gas station. Or the handyman the landlord sends over after your sink has been backed up for a week. He did not look like he was capable of doing something like that to a nineteen-year-old girl. But I have also learned there is a breed of white man in the South who can have you weeping alongside him over a glass of beer and can slit your throat from ear to ear all in the same night.

I told him who I was and asked if he would talk to me. I said he didn't have to if he didn't want to.

"I'll talk to you," he said. "I'll talk to anybody ain't made up their mind I done it."

"All right," I began. "*Did* you do it?"

"No sir," he said with a convulsive shake of his head. "I never laid a hand on that girl."

"Why do the police think you did?"

"They don't think nothing," he sneered. "They're trying to hang it on me 'cause they got nobody better." He leaned forward and spat into the coffee can.

"But you knew her," I pointed out, "and you were seen in the restaurant the day she was killed."

He swallowed and I could see his Adam's apple move up and then down at the front of his throat. "I had one beer that afternoon — I done told the police that."

"They said you'd stopped by her trailer before, that you'd been chased off from there."

I couldn't decide whether that made him scared or angry. His face didn't change, but his eyes now were like sharp-edged pieces of gravel. He pressed against the corner as if I'd backed him into it. Then he made an effort and gathered himself together. He began to talk in a slow, deliberate monotone. "I was driving by, and I'd had a few beers, and I seen her getting out of the car, and I stopped. It wudn't but a mile down the road from the restaurant. So I pulled off onto the gravel and I stopped. All I did was call her name and some guy come tearing out like he was gonna take my head off. Look," he said, "is that a crime?"

"I don't know," I said. "Maybe it is."

"Listen, mister, I'll tell you the truth. I didn't even tell the police this," he went on. "She was just a little bit of a tease. You know, nothing real bad. She'd lean over more than she needed to when she sat the beer down, and she'd kinda twitch her butt at me when she walked away." He stopped as if he was remembering that. "Enough to keep me coming back in for a beer once in a while. But I never so much as laid a hand on her — that's the gospel truth. She just must have waved it oncet in front of the wrong dude, that's all."

He kept his voice flat, but a slight leer crept into his eyes, and I had a momentary urge to slap him across the face. I don't know why. It passed quickly. After a minute he asked, "Don't you believe me?"

I said, "What about the girl down in Mobile?"

He smiled for the first time since I had walked in, showing bad teeth. "You ever heard of a man getting sent over 'cause a fifteen-year-old gal can't keep her pants up?"

"Okay," I said, standing up to go. As I was standing there, he said, "When you write my story, I hope you'll tell the truth, mister. That's your job."

Nobody was ever going to write his story, I thought. And if he believed my job was telling the truth — well, the poor bastard.

I saw Harris on the way out. He smiled and said, "Did ya get you a full confession?"

I smiled back. "Some suspect," I said. "I'll have to write something for McDermott."

He frowned and said in his official voice: "We're holding someone in connection with the murder of Fonda Lyn Trafford. No formal charges filed yet." He nodded curtly at me. "You ought to get two pages out of that."

When I walked into the city room, McDermott looked up as if he fully expected me to toss a signed confession, neatly typed, across his desk. "Well?" he said.

I told him what I'd learned. And I added, "If you ask me, the guy's just some redneck who happened to be handy. I don't think he had anything to do with it."

"Congratulations," he said. "Four months on police beat and already you've made detective."

I looked toward the ceiling. He tapped his finger on the desk. "This may come as a surprise to you, Phillips, but our readers aren't particularly interested in what you think. They're interested in what the police think. And we pay you to report that to them. So just write it the way they told it to you."

I sat down at the typewriter and caught Henry Slidell smirking at me out of the side of his face. I started to tell him to go find someone to expose himself in front of, but thought better of it. While I was typing, Bob Hurlbut came back to my desk.

"We're going to Sammy's tonight after work," he said. "Care to come along? They've got a new dancer with lovely features," and he cradled his hands out in front of him.

"Let you know later."

"Don't mind McDermott," he told me. "If he really thought you were going to fuck up, he'd have someone else on it by now."

When I handed in the story, McDermott didn't say a word. It ran the next morning with the girl's picture again. Two days later they released Franklin because of insufficient evidence, and the police were no closer to solving the case than they had been before. Except that, as Harris said, "That's one redneck son-of-a-bitch I can cross off the list. There can't be more than fifty thousand of 'em left in this county to investigate."

Other than that, it was a slow week and I wrote more than my share of obituaries. On Thursday I stopped by Cassie's father's to get some books she had asked me to pick up. His office was in a 1920s skyscraper downtown. I rather liked going by there; I liked talking to Mr. Fairchild or listening to him, particularly when no one else was around, not even Cassie.

In some ways Mr. Fairchild reminded me of my own father. As a Mississippi newspaper editor, my father had won prizes but lost readers and eventually the paper shut down. Afterwards, he came to Birmingham and joined an advertising agency. But his heart was never in it. I believe he did it mainly for my mother — like my grandfather, he felt he had failed his family, and he hadn't even the excuse of a poor cotton crop. As a would-be political reformer, Mr. Fairchild had suffered the same fate that my father had as a newspaper editor — they were both noble failures — and I suppose I admired each of them for it.

Mr. Fairchild was busy when I arrived that morning; a low relentless buzz of voices came from the inner office. I was trying to decide whether to wait when I noticed a boyish figure sitting on the floor, leaning against a bookcase, his knees drawn up and his eyes apparently closed. He had a slight build with delicate features and light hair, a little long in the back, and for some reason I couldn't stop staring at him. He opened his eyes like he'd known all along I was there and stared back, a stare that was part curious and part baleful.

Then he made a gesture of his head, as if he were shaking some hair out of his face, although there was none in it. And I realized why I was looking at him. Cassie made the same gesture if she was nervous or impatient and wanted to hide it. I could see the image of Cassie also around his eyes and mouth, except that in him the prettiness was out of place. There were faint moon-shaped scars across his face, where some childhood disease must have left its mark.

I said, "You must be Timmy."

He smiled at first, a liquid smile that was continually melting away and re-forming, then his eyes retreated a little, as if they were threatened. "How do you know who I am?"

"You look like your sister," I said.

A glimmer of the smile came back. "So you're Cassie's beau, huh, man?" He said it with a disarming innocence that almost obscured the sneer behind it, but not quite.

"Yes," I said.

"I've never seen you around the house," he said.

"I don't get up there too often."

He laughed unexpectedly. "Neither do I."

I pulled up a chair and waited for Mr. Fairchild. Timmy was clearly waiting for something, too, and we had an awkward, intermittent conversation. His behavior toward me was by turns arrogant and deferential. And I thought there was something likable about him, although perhaps it was merely something pitiable.

When Mr. Fairchild appeared, he nodded at me and said, "Hello, Nick," then turned to his son. "Sorry, Timmy, I'll be with you in a minute. Your mother and I had business." He was holding open the inner office door, and a woman walked out. I don't know what I had expected. Considering all I had heard, anything short of a winged harpy should have been disappointing. But Mrs. Fairchild was rather tall and imposing-looking. In fact, she must, as Melissa had put it, have been pretty once. And again I saw the family resemblance, although with her it was not defined in any single feature. But my overwhelming impression was that everything about her — the angles of her face, even the folds of her dress — had been chiseled with tremendous effort out of some terribly unyielding piece of stone.

I stood up.

"Julia," Mr. Fairchild said, "this is Nick Phillips."

She lifted her head and stretched her arm to me, fingers extended, palm downward.

"I've heard a great deal about you, Nick. I'm sorry my daughter has not yet found the opportunity to introduce us properly. I must apologize for her lack of consideration."

"That's all right," I said, wondering whom she had heard about me from. "I'm sure there's nothing to apologize for."

She looked at me for just a second, as if she was making up her mind about something. Then she said, "I hope you will come to the house sometime. We're giving a little party next weekend; I shall insist that Cassie bring you along." She turned to Timmy. "Will I see *you* at the house this week?"

He shrugged and then gave her that liquid smile. "Guess so."

Mr. Fairchild walked her out into the hall. I heard Timmy say, "Well, what do you think of Mama?"

"She seems pleasant enough." It sounded lame, but it was all I could think of to say.

He chuckled. "She's a little stiff, but she's okay. If you don't cross her," he added.

I frowned at him.

"Cheer up, man," he said with a grin. "I think she likes you."

Mr. Fairchild strode purposefully back across the room to the desk, sat down, and leaned back with his hands behind his head. "All right, Timmy, what can I do for *you*?"

Timmy was still leaning against the bookcase, and his eyes were beginning to look closed again. "It's just some money I owe a guy. I thought maybe you could loan it to me."

"You wanted five hundred dollars in June," Mr. Fairchild said, looking through his checkbook. "How much is it this time?"

"I don't know," he said as if he were haggling over the price of a piece of furniture. "Four hundred and fifty dollars."

Mr. Fairchild gave a very short laugh. "That's a bit too much."

Timmy shrugged. "Three-fifty."

"All right," his father said pleasantly. He wrote the check, tore it off and laid it on the desk, but kept his index finger over it. "I hope you won't owe any more guys for the next few months. Understood."

"Over and out," Timmy said, taking the check and crumpling it into his back jeans pocket with a slight swagger. As he walked away he turned toward me and said, in a mincing voice with a nasal twang to it, "Maybe Cassie can bring you along to one of my little parties sometime." Then he was out the door.

Mr. Fairchild leaned even farther back in the chair, gave a long sigh and said "Jesus" all in the same breath.

"Today was payday." He smiled wryly at me. "He comes in whenever he needs cash; I don't even want to know where it goes anymore." He sighed again. "It doesn't matter. I know he gets three times the amount from his mother that he gets from me. In fact, I'm convinced he only comes here now on principle — he believes it is the one filial obligation he can live up to: he can keep on taking my money." Mr. Fairchild shook his head. "Forgive my cynicism; it is simply that the older I get, the less I understand about anybody, particularly my own children. What is it that makes anyone child or father to anyone else? Merely some infinitesimal speck of a gene, a biological compulsion in the blood? Like sex," he went on almost to himself, "purely a male, or female, hormonal imperative. We are the most intricate of mechanisms, and also the simplest. Well," he said dryly, turning back to me, "so much for the lecture on biology and metaphysics. I'll save religion till tomorrow."

ten

Although Mr. and Mrs. Fairchild scarcely managed to live together in the same house, they regularly gave the grandest and most elaborate parties in the city. Once, sometimes twice a month, the whole place blazed with lights, and enough Birmingham police to quell a small riot were on hand to direct the cars that came cruising like yachts up the long brick driveway.

The parties, I learned later, were Mrs. Fairchild's means of maintaining her position in town. She kept herself at the center of things, surrounded by large numbers of influential people. And in exchange for a fund-raising affair at the Fairchild home each year, she received a place on the museum board or the Beaux Arts Ball committee or whatever else she was after. Mr. Fairchild's motives were not so clear. I suppose he acted the host to preserve what he could of domestic tranquillity; perhaps he even told himself he was helping to make a home for his children. But I suspect he secretly enjoyed being the dispenser of the city's most lavish and celebrated hospitality. There was within him a regard for convention that would have horrified him had he realized the full extent of it. With Julia he didn't have to. Instead he could preside over her parties, welcoming everyone from the Friends of the Museum to the Virginal Daughters of the Confederacy. And at the same time, he could play the part of the cynical world-weary host, retreating to his library whenever the party bored him, occasionally saying or doing something a little bit shocking.

Maybe I'm being too hard on him. Yet those parties don't evoke my fondest memories of anybody. And then I come to ask myself why I went, not just once but several times. Did I go for the same reason Mr. Fairchild played host, because I wanted to preserve some measure of tranquillity between Cassie and me? But she only insisted that first night, after her mother — as good as her word — had issued the invitation. When I asked why she wanted to go, she gave me a serious look and said, "I have my reasons, you wouldn't understand." And she was right, I didn't understand. But I went, not only for Cassie but out of some deep-seated and dubious fascination of my own, and I didn't completely understand that either.

Mrs. Fairchild's parties were an unchanging backdrop against which that summer and fall unfolded. And except for certain events of the last evening, it is difficult for me to separate them in my mind. Close to five hundred people must have walked through the doors of that house each time, and only a handful of them stand out, often for trivial reasons. A frail blond named Bitsy announced one night that she had undergone a religious conversion, then stripped naked and stepped into a goldfish pond. Three unmarried sisters, aging debutantes, came with their mother, and no matter how warm it was all four of them wore platinum mink stoles and hair to match. Hubert "Boonie" Lathrop, the anti-abortion congressman, brought along Connie Rawls, the gospel singer who'd founded the Holy Family Alliance. An elderly woman with brilliant white hair was said to have had her right nipple bitten off during a party in the twenties at the old Country Club of Birmingham. And there was a tall woman with an

79

undefinable accent who called herself a ballet mistress. Later someone told me she ran the most lucrative call girl operation in three states.

But the great majority of the guests were less conspicuous — prominent businessmen, bankers, lawyers, and their wives. The homegrown variety of southern millionaire. Solid beefy men like Gritt Lackey, chairman of a bank holding company, and Mason "Pump" Farlowe, president of the Great South Power Company. I had heard a story at the *Examiner* about Farlowe — that years ago a grand jury had come within one vote of indicting him for the murder of his first wife. His current wife, Lady B. Farlowe, seemed blissfully ignorant of any such homicidal possibilities. There were a few foreigners also, attesting to the New South's conviction that money can be cultivated in the most exotic of climates. Frank Hammond, the coal magnate, brought along two South Africans and a Japanese businessman who, he said, was nephew to the emperor. One night there was even an Arab oil sheik, looking more like a southern planter, in a white linen suit and Panama hat above his black beard. He came with Crawford Jamison, who had served in the last Republican cabinet and whose "little construction company" was presently building an air base in the Saudi Arabian desert.

And I remember one old man who must have been past eighty; he could barely hear and walked, if he walked at all, with a cane in one hand and two blond girls on either arm, although I do not believe he ever came with the same pair twice. This was Asa Hammer, the oldest partner in Hammer, Glove, Fairchild, the law firm Cassie's grandfather had helped to found. There were also, sprinkled among the guests, young couples nearly our own age. Privately I thought of these as promising young hopefuls — junior partners and executives on their way up, their wives the same girls I had seen at the debutante party, only a little older, a bit more disheveled, and, sometimes by the end of the evening, a good deal drunker. It was quite a plum for a young man to be invited to a Fairchild party — a sort of badge that great things were expected of him, inside the firm and out. The first time I walked in with Cassie on my arm, several of these young men regarded me with suspicion and a certain amount of envy.

The last and grandest of these parties was held at the end of September. It was an annual affair called "Stars Fall on Alabama," cosponsored by the Civic Opera Guild, of which Melissa was a board member. Melissa was actually the one who first suggested we go. "It'll be a hoot," she said to us one night, "fireworks and everything." It took me a few minutes to realize that she was in fact dreading it but had determined to put in an appearance. Perhaps she thought our presence would render hers less conspicuous, or maybe she wanted us along for moral support. Cassie shook some imaginary curl out of her eyes, smiled, and said, "Why of course we'll go," although I was certain she did not want to. And I was equally sure she wasn't being agreeable merely as a favor to Melissa. As for me, I said I thought it sounded terrific. I think I had made up my mind to show Cassie that I could be just as stubbornly perverse as she could. If that was what I was trying to prove, I was wrong.

That evening revealed a clear blue-black sky dotted with stars, as if the entire galaxy had been catered for the Fairchild party. It was still warm, but the warmth was the remnant of another season, and, as the night wore on, it vanished into thin air. The house was fully lit and visible blocks away. Even the air around it glittered with miniature electric bulbs strung through the tops of trees. Yet it did not look as imposing to me as it had that night months ago when my headlights swept up the long curving drive for the first time. And as I drove up with Cassie beside me to attend her parents' party,

I felt that I had finally come full circle and was only now about to discover the place I had started from.

We got out, and I handed the keys to a gray-uniformed attendant. A butler I had never seen before opened the door, and five steps inside we were met by a waiter carrying a tray of champagne. Cassie told me later that her parents hired half the staff of Shady Vale Country Club for a party such as this. The house was more crowded than I had ever seen it. It took us thirty minutes and three glasses of champagne to get through the hallway. The party was spread all over the place, but most of the noise was coming from downstairs.

A stone stairway descended to the Norman Room, the cavernous medieval-looking hall complete with high arching windows, granite walls, and vaulted ceiling. Wine and beer flowed from large wooden kegs. Against one wall stood a long table laden with fruits, loaves of bread, whole cheeses, and in the midst of everything a roast suckling pig, apple crammed into its mouth as if it had died swallowing it. The room was warm and crowded with revelers, and we walked on through to the patio.

Beyond the patio lay a rich carpet of grass that had the uniformity and consistency of a slow court at Wimbledon. It stretched all the way to a low stone wall that literally crowned the ridge of Red Mountain. And beyond that was nothing but the still night air and the lights of the city blinking far beneath our feet. At one end of this terrace was a brightly lit fountain, a fine spray of mist hanging over it like a halo. The orchestra sat on a platform behind the fountain, rising above the mist as if out of a cloud, mingling big-band music with a little brassy rock and roll.

At the other end was the bar. I saw Cassie's father leaning against it with a glass in his hand, while not far off her mother chatted easily with some of their guests. Mr. Fairchild wore a tuxedo jacket above a pair of gray trousers and a faintly ironic smile that flickered for an instant into one of pleasure when he caught our eye.

I touched Cassie's elbow. "Let's go speak to your parents."

We started in their direction. Mrs. Fairchild picked us out and gave us a distant smile, as if she were standing much farther away than thirty feet. Her tall figure was sheathed in a long, rather closely fitting pale silk dress, and her hair was swept up behind a diamond choker at her throat.

Mrs. Fairchild was always gracious to me in a formal sort of way. She gave me her hand and said, "I'm so pleased you could come tonight." She kissed Cassie on the cheek, then stepped back, fingertips resting lightly on her daughter's shoulders, and looked her appraisingly up and down. At last she pronounced, "I don't like beige on you. I think a darker color would show your skin to better advantage, especially if you insist on wearing it that low in front."

Mr. Fairchild was standing by with the same amused smile, his head bent slightly, as if even outside there were dangerously low doorways everywhere. "Are you two enjoying our little party?" he asked.

"It's some little party," I answered.

"We like it," he said. "But we enjoy simple pleasures; all we ask is to be surrounded by a few close friends and our children on a night like this. Isn't that so, Julia?" Her expression never changed, and without waiting for an answer, he gave her his arm, and they turned back to their guests. But he called over his shoulder, "Make sure you stick around for the fireworks."

"Daddy's just showing off because you're here," Cassie said with distaste.

I took that as something of a compliment, although I didn't tell her so.

A waiter passed, and I reached more champagne out of the air. I downed a couple of glasses while Cassie did little more than stare at hers, twirling the stem in her fingers.

"Do you want to dance?" I asked her.

"Sure," she said, "why not?" as if it were a novel idea.

We hadn't danced since that night at the country club, and I had forgotten how charged her body felt beneath my fingers. We moved easily across the terrace to a waltz-time number, the air around me pulsing with a small exquisite current of electricity. The orchestra played two more slow songs, then launched into rhythm and blues, an old Aretha Franklin number sung by a young black woman with a powerful rough-hewn voice.

In the middle of the dance I felt a tap on my shoulder and turned to see a man a few years older and a few inches taller grinning down at me. I recognized him as one of the young hopefuls who had stared the first time I walked into a party with Cassie. "Do you mind, old buddy?" he said. I minded his calling me old buddy, but I stepped to the side. He put his arm around Cassie's waist; however, before he could take a step, she insisted on introducing us.

"Nick, this is Rud Bearden," she said, with that amused look on her face. "Nick Phillips." We shook hands. He had blond hair and a light brick-colored complexion. By this time the song had ended, and Rud looked uncertain about whether to make conversation. Finally he asked what I did. I told him, and he said that sounded interesting, did I plan on making a career of it. He himself was with the Great South Power Company. I was tempted to ask him about Mason Farlowe's first wife, but I didn't. Instead I excused myself and said I was going to the bar. "Bring me something," Cassie asked. As I walked away, the orchestra began to play and Rud broke into a stiff, tentative jitterbug.

I strolled the length of the terrace, enjoying the sights and sounds of the party, feeling almost lighthearted for the first time that evening. At the bar I ordered drinks, then wandered back through the crowd sipping a scotch, balancing a full vodka collins in my other hand. Scraps of conversations drifted by me. Men swapping stock-market tips while their wives listened. 'Bama fans talking serious football — "We've got some damn good niggers down there this year, but I'd trade 'em all to have the Bear back."

A woman waved at me from the patio. I stared for a full minute before I recognized Melissa, looking uncharacteristically subdued in a simple black evening dress and white gloves. I walked over, glad for a chance to talk to someone, and set the drinks down.

"Hello, love," she said. "Do you know Jess?" She indicated a big man standing beside her who looked like a country lawyer. Jess smiled and offered a large comfortable hand.

He asked me if I was Sam Phillips's son, and I said yes.

"Your father was a good man," he said. "We worked together in the sixties." "The sixties" meant civil-rights work. Jess said it as if he was neither bragging about it nor trying to live it down. "Fine man," he repeated. He turned to Melissa with a mock bow. "Madame, may I offer you some liquid refreshment?"

"Why I thought you'd never ask," she answered. "Jess is sweet," she told me after he'd ambled off toward the bar. "He's a bankruptcy judge." I hadn't been too far off. "I asked him to bring me tonight so I'd look respectable." She fingered her dress. "What do you think? Does it look like it's right off the rack at the Salvation Army?"

I laughed. "You look respectable enough for a funeral."

"Well, shut my mouth," Melissa said. "Here comes the dragon lady of respectability herself."

Mrs. Fairchild was walking toward us, her chin lifted, her face composed into a smooth economical smile.

"So nice to see you, Melissa." She held her hand out at arm's length. "I wasn't at all sure you would be able to come tonight." And for the first time I thought I heard the trace of a south-Georgia accent in her voice.

"Why, Julia," Melissa said with bland surprise. "The devil himself couldn't keep me away from one of your parties. Or the pope either," she added irreverently.

"I'm so glad. Perhaps we'll have a chance to talk later," she said, gliding away to greet someone else.

At that moment Jess returned from the bar. Melissa took a deep breath, said, "Cheers," and turned her glass bottom up.

I had a couple of drinks with Jess and Melissa, then found myself leaning alone against a marble-topped table, sipping the vodka collins I had been carrying around. It tasted watery and sweet. I tried to pick Cassie out among the dancers, but from here they were no more than a distant blur of moving shapes.

The next thing I knew, she was walking toward me from the other side of the terrace. "Where have you been?"

"Went to get you a drink," I told her, holding up what was left of the vodka collins, "and I ran into Melissa. What happened to ol' brick Rud?"

"How should I know?" she said, looking around. "Where is Melissa?"

"She's here somewhere," I said. "She came with a bank-ruptcy judge."

Cassie laughed. "You mean Jess." She gazed at me and wrinkled her forehead. "Are you all right?"

"Absolutely," I answered. "Who is Rud anyway?"

"He's not anybody," she said. "He's an old boyfriend."

"Old brick, old beau," I said, enjoying the sound of it.

She regarded me more closely. "I think you're a little drunk."

I said, "Hmmm," as if thinking that over. Cassie took my arm, although I felt quite steady, and we walked out onto the terrace, away from the dancing. It must have been close to twelve o'clock, because the fireworks were set for midnight, and the next thing I knew, I was looking up as the night sky reeled with great phosphorescent wheels of fire, Roman candles bursting like dazzling umbrellas overhead. For a few seconds it looked as if Mr. and Mrs. Fairchild had succeeded in calling the stars down for one brief spectacular show. Then I remember thinking of my father taking me to the Alabama State Fair, and of stumbling sleepily across the mud-crusted field to the car as the night came to a close with a crescendo of fireworks.

After that I lost track of time completely. I felt as if I were sitting in the front seat of a roller coaster that had been inching upward all night and now was plunging down a long, long incline. It was an unusual roller coaster, because nothing was blurred; in fact, sometimes the people around me appeared to move in slow motion. But scene after scene rushed past me with no apparent connection and no coherence at all.

We are standing on the patio with Mrs. Fairchild, and I am trying to concentrate while she introduces me to Asa Hammer. He isn't leaning on the arms of his blond girls anymore; it looks like he is leaning on Cassie's arm. He is speaking partly to me, and I catch bits of phrases, ". . . very fortunate young man . . . like a granddaughter to me . . . you will permit me, my dear." He leans over and I think he is going to kiss Cassie on the cheek, but he kisses her instead on the mouth. He has bright hawk eyes and a forehead as frail and translucent as an eggshell. The orchestra strikes up a number, and he beats time with his cane.

More introductions. A young lawyer in the same firm, wearing club tie, firm jaw, and broad smile. How do you do? he asks. How did you manage this? he means. There is another man named Peal, or Steel, or something. He is older, more imposing-looking, with eyes the color of his slate gray suit. His mouth scarcely opens when he speaks. ". . . absolutely invaluable to me," Mrs. Fairchild is saying. "Gets things done," Asa Hammer says, "all my dirty work," and he winks, for some reason, at me. Someone whispers — it must have been Cassie — "he's Mama's lawyer."

I am somewhere inside the house. For just a second I think it is the library, but I am sitting in a plain ladder-back chair, a kitchen chair, listening to Mr. Fairchild. Although we are sitting at the same table, his voice seems muffled and distant, as if it carries to me out of a long sad hallway. A couple comes giggling and crashing through, looking for more ice. They stop to gawk at me and this middle-aged man in a tuxedo jacket hunched over the kitchen table, and they laugh louder, thinking probably that he is trying to sober up before driving home. I want to stand and tell these people that this is their host, that it is his liquor they are drinking, his fireworks they are dancing under; but he dismisses guests, orchestras, fireworks, he dismisses the entire pleasure-seeking world with a wave of his hand. "We must be," he says, "the most curious and unlikely creatures who have ever walked this earth, far more so than the dinosaurs, who after all survived for several hundred million years. After we have first elevated biology into poetry, we reduce it to the merest, most brutal debauchery. And then we try to live or die in the name of it. Have you," he suddenly asks me, "ever been in love?"

Cassie and I are dancing again. She looks, if anything, more stunning than she has all evening. It is very late. Some of the musicians appear half-asleep, but they are still playing, and the black singer slowly unburdens herself of an undulating blues tune, "What you going to do when I'm gone, bay-b-a-y, what you going to do when I'm gone?" A young woman, using all fours, climbs up onto the wall at the edge of the terrace. She has been trying all night to get her husband's attention, and now she stands and clasps her hands above her head. The orchestra obliges with a desultory bump and grind. She weaves and sways and begins to strip off her dress. She has her husband's attention.

I am still light-headed, but my private roller coaster is easing now into a long smooth straightaway. Cassie gives my arm a little tug. "Come with me," she whispers.

I feel as if I have been pushed and pulled in different directions all evening and I stand my ground. "Where are we going?"

"I want to show you something. A secret." She looks coy — more than coy, she looks mysterious.

"What?"

"If I tell you it won't be a secret anymore." She pouts, as if I am a child whose stubbornness is spoiling the fun. Dropping my arm, she turns and half-runs across the terrace. I follow in spite of myself, catching up, a little out of breath, in the Norman Room. It is empty except for the roast pig lying spilled open on the table, half-eaten, apple still intact. Beneath the stone stairs Cassie opens a small door to what looks like a broom closet. She pushes against the inside wall, and it swings slowly into a black open doorway with Cassie outlined against it. She smiles and motions for me to follow. For a moment I wonder if I am trapped inside a bad movie. But I have come this far. She shuts the panel behind us, and we are in utter darkness.

"What is this?" I feel a small quick spurt of adrenaline.

"No castle would be complete without its secret passage," she says.

"Where is the maiden in distress?" I ask.

In answer she kisses me. I put my arms around her and brush across cobwebs as thick as a string mop. "Christ." I jump back. "Has anyone been in here in the past ten years?"

She switches on a naked bulb hanging from a bare wire above a steep cramped stairway. We are at the bottom and it is a long way up. "This was my great-grandfather's idea. When he built this place, he made them put it in because he said you weren't rich until you owned a house with a secret passage. But I think it was just his nature — being secretive and deceptive," she says. "Timmy and I used to play here when we were little."

"Where does it go?"

"Come see."

We climb to the landing, and I see that the stairs turn up another flight. "We're right behind the kitchen now," she tells me, moving back. "Push."

Feeling a little silly, I press against the wall — tentatively at first, as if it will push back, then harder, with both hands — and it moves, squeaking, swinging slowly, heavily outward. No wonder. I am standing in the pantry, and the wall is laden with a rich array of canned goods — soups, vegetables, oblong tins of exotic meats, spices whose names I can only guess at. One can of Spanish artichoke hearts has toppled off and rolled out onto the kitchen floor. I step back quickly, as if I am afraid of being caught pilfering the vichyssoise or Alaskan crab legs.

"There's more up here," Cassie says.

"What," I ask, "a raving hunchback who lives off spiders?"

"Hush," she tells me. "We're almost to the top. I used to be afraid to come this far." Her voice is scarcely more than a whisper. "This opens to what was originally the master bedroom. It's at the other end of the house from the main stairs, and it must have been handy for quick exits."

"Yes," I answer, trying to bring myself back to earth, "or midnight snacks." The stairs have ended in a tiny space just high enough to stand up in. The light does not reach all the way up and I can barely see her.

"Get a load of this." She shoots back a little panel, and a pinprick of light pierces the wall. "Daddy had it put in as a joke. He said no secret passage was worthy of the name without a spyhole. It's right behind a portrait of my great-great grandfather." She steps back. "Go on, take a look."

I have to bend over to get on eye level with it, and a new wave of dizziness washes over me, more gentle than before but just as insistent. So at first my eyes do not focus. It is like looking through the wrong end of a telescope: I see the bedroom, long and narrow, as if it is moving away from me, and the two of us are behind the wall at one end of it. At the opposite end, jutting out from the wall, I see a large canopied bed with a white lace coverlet. The yellow globe of a table lamp casts a pale amber light over half the room. And on the side of the bed, outlined vividly against the white coverlet, I see Mrs. Fairchild sitting — perfectly naked except for the diamonds at her throat. Someone else is on the bed also, but he does not come into full view until he leans over her from behind and presses his lips against her shoulder. Without turning around she reaches back and puts her hand to his face, and her breast lifts and firms for a second like a young girl's; then she drops her arm and sags back into the flaccid form of a middle-aged woman. I cannot get a good look at the man's face, but I know he is much younger than she. In the amber light, the entire scene looks like an old photograph, or an oil painting that has been hidden away somewhere, one that has yellowed and darkened with age. Suddenly she swings her body around to embrace him, and for a second all of her — belly, breasts, shoulders, eyes — faces squarely where I am. Her head lifts and I shiver, catching a faint hint of

Cassie there. But there is no hint of anyone in the expression of her face; she wears a bright, cold, fixed smile, as if that can mask everything — age, death, even desire. And I almost believe it is an oil painting, some sixteenth-century master's vision of age masquerading as youth, of beauty transformed by corruption. As they embrace I turn away.

I straightened up and stepped back from the wall. I was still dizzy, and there were unwelcome tremors running up and down my legs. But the vision of Mrs. Fairchild had had a palpable effect on me, as if it were a quick sharp slap to the face. I willed myself to have a clear head.

Cassie closed the panel and asked, in a good-humored voice, "Did you see anything interesting?"

I looked at her. Up here in the dark her face was even less clearly defined to me than her mother's had been. I wondered whether she had any idea of what I'd just seen, and I was not certain I wanted to find out. But if she had, she gave no hint of it. And the last thing I intended to do was tell her. "A nice four-poster bed," I answered.

"Oh, the bed," Cassie said as we started down, "it belonged to my father's mother."

I heard a distant saxophone when we stepped out of the passage — no band behind it, just a clear lone alto sax. The orchestra was packing up, and what guests remained had gravitated toward the bar. Compared to a few hours ago, the terrace was a vast empty space, the sky no longer reeling but still and empty, too. The sax player stood and played softly to himself, as if he preferred no other audience but the moon and the quiet stars. I thought about the evening Cassie and I had listened together to Ben Tiner's saxophone and how far we had come since then, and I wondered how far we had yet to go.

From somewhere not too far off the sound of sirens mingled with the saxophone's song. A faint acrid odor in the air reminded me a little of the smell of the steel mills the night I had driven to Hueytown.

"I wonder what's happening," Cassie said. A crowd was gathering near the wall at the end of the terrace.

"I don't know," I said. "You mean this isn't on the program, after the fireworks and the house tour?"

"No." She shook her head.

There were enough guests left to fill the area between the bar and the stone wall where it formed a corner at one end. By this time of night they were either very drunk or trying hard to be, and the revelry threatened to turn to ugliness at any moment. People were jostling and shoving, as if they wanted to get a better view of something. "What's going on?" I asked, struggling to make my way through with Cassie behind me. "I'm always the last to find out," said a man near me, his hands around the chest of the woman in front of him. She was holding a champagne bottle, almost empty, and she said, "Have a drink, honey," either to me or to him. I turned sideways and tried to wedge my shoulder forward. It was like pushing through some faintly organic material that gives way slowly but without resistance and then closes in behind you. An arm struck out and something sharp — a fingernail or a ring — stung my cheek.

Near the front I heard a voice say, "Spectacular," and someone else echoed, "Better than the fireworks." I pushed on through, elbowing a squat man who said, "Oomph," but I didn't slow to apologize. When I got close enough to look over the wall, I saw a spreading column of thick dark smoke hanging in the air. Shrouded by the smoke, sporadic flames leapt out of a building halfway down the mountain, momentarily illuminating what they fed upon. Skeletons of walls showed themselves transparent before the fire; the ghost of a stairwell dropped in a slow concave arch, vanishing before it touched the floor.

A newcomer asked, "Where is it — what's burning?"

"Highlands clubhouse," someone answered, "not much left now."

"Hell of an eyesore," a voice behind me said. "Save the city the cost of tearing it down."

I looked at it for several minutes; the smoke was beginning to drift slowly, heavily away from us northward. A few people were turning back to whatever the excitement had interrupted. The man with his hands around the woman in front of him was nuzzling the back of her neck, while she stared straight ahead into the drifting smoke. And I overheard a middle-aged man, whom I thought I recognized as Gritt Lackey, whisper to a well-built blond, the wife of one of the young hopefuls, "Honey, I got me a fire that's gon' be hard to put out tonight." He laid a beefy hand on her buttocks; her husband looked in the other direction. I looked around suddenly for Cassie; but she was nowhere in sight, and I pushed my way rather roughly out of the crowd back toward the house.

I stopped for a minute where the dancers had been, looking back at the entire scene, and I noticed one couple alone a little way off from the crowd. All I could make out was the outline of their heads and shoulders against the vaguely lit sky, but I knew instinctively who they were. I moved closer. Mr. Fairchild stood with his hands in his pockets and his head bent forward in a sort of dignified slouch. Beside him Melissa just looked, mouth opened a little, with the innocent amazement of a child. She noticed me first. "There you are, love," she said with a bright strained gaiety. "Have you seen the fire?"

"Yes, I was watching it," I answered.

"It's just about finished now," she said, turning back as if it were the drawn-out finale of an Italian opera she had to watch right to the end.

Mr. Fairchild turned on me with a desolate look, a look of almost inconsolable disappointment tempered only by the suggestion that it must have been after all inevitable. "What a sad waste," he said. And I realized that Melissa had spoken almost exactly the same words to me the night I had seen her at Highlands.

Someone nearby said in apparent agreement. "Quite a place in its time." It was Jess, Melissa's escort. "Of course it hadn't been kept up. It's a wonder it held up this long."

By now the fire department had arrived in force. But the building was too far gone, and they looked like actors in a silent movie making absurdly comical gestures. When they trained their hoses on it, bright yellow flames rose higher, and a small mock cheer went up from the crowd near us. I turned around, and it was then that I recognized Cassie caught up among them. She stood motionless, like a deer transfixed by the glare of an oncoming car. And as that fitful light wavered across her face, it took shape anew for me: the high cheekbones that threw her deep eyes into relief, the full curving mouth parted slightly. There was an upward lilt to her entire face as if she were looking not into the fire but beyond it.

I shouldered back through the crowd and grabbed hold of her arm. I had to shake her before she became aware of me. "Come on," I said. "Let's get out of here, let's go home." She looked up bewildered, and I could feel her arm trembling.

A man leered at me. "If I was you," he said, "I'd be in a hurry to get home, too." Then Cassie nodded and allowed me to pull her out of the crowd's grasp.

Melissa and Mr. Fairchild were standing exactly as I had left them, with Jess now beside them. I told Melissa we were leaving and she said, "Good night, love," but kept staring straight ahead. I shook hands with Jess. Cassie walked around in front of her father and stood on tiptoes and kissed him. He looked at her somberly, and I remembered what I had thought the first time I saw them together, that there was some secret understanding between them.

We didn't go back through the house. Instead we walked the entire length of the terrace, then followed a serpentine path through the garden to the driveway. Once I looked back at the dwindling knot of spectators, and I saw far behind them on the patio the lone figure of a woman, hands clasped in front of her and head raised. It might have been Mrs. Fairchild, but I couldn't tell for sure.

eleven

*A*ll the way down the driveway our footsteps echoed off the bricks — hard glazed stones from some old Confederate furnace, Cassie had told me once. One cop was still out front leaning against a car, a black Lincoln sporting a MORAL MAJORITY bumper sticker. He straightened when he saw us. My Chevrolet was parked a long way off, and we walked toward it without saying a word. Cassie got in on my side and slid over. After I had started the engine and pulled out, she said, "I don't want to go back to Melissa's tonight."

"All right," I said. We drove past a few other cars, scattered like empty hulls along the side of the road, and past the driveway to the house. The last I saw of it were the electric lights winking at me out of the tops of the trees.

"It's hateful," she burst out after a moment. "I couldn't bear to live like that."

"To live like what?" I couldn't help asking.

But she didn't answer me. Instead she said, "Sometimes I try to imagine what it would be like if Daddy had married differently. Do you ever do that? I wonder who I would be then." She paused. "But I wouldn't be at all, would I? Someone else would." She gave a little shivery laugh that made me flinch. "I suppose that must be the most perfect form of suicide in the world," she said. "If you could go back in time and stop your parents before there was ever a chance for you to be born."

I didn't have an answer to that. But I had seen and heard a lot that evening that I didn't have any answer to. I tightened my grip on the steering wheel and concentrated on guiding the car down the narrow twisting road, hugging the shoulder whenever a pair of headlights swung toward us. We drove along the ridge past stately old homes, silent and sleeping peacefully, with no hint of the dark and private lives raging within them. Then we wound down the slope close to town where the houses were just as old and showed it more, past the inroads of new apartment complexes with Spanish-sounding names, and finally I pulled into the dead-end street where my building stood between two run-down examples of antebellum revival.

Neither of us spoke as we got out of the car. I took Cassie's hand — it seemed an awkwardly self-conscious gesture — and we walked in silence across the courtyard, then climbed the stairs to my apartment. She leaned against the wrought-iron railing, while I fumbled with the key. "God, I'm so tired," she said, throwing her head back and yawning lazily. My legs felt like they were set in concrete. The key slid in, and the bolt clicked open. "I'm tired enough to sleep for three days," she repeated.

Tired wasn't what I felt; I was simply exhausted, used up. But I didn't want to go straight to bed. To have something to do I walked through the living room into the kitchen and switched on the lamp over the sink. The alarm clock on the counter said ten minutes past four. There was a faint sweet smell coming from the corner where I had neglected to empty the garbage. I was suddenly grateful for a reason to go back outside. I knotted the top of the plastic bag and picked it up, can and all. "Be back in a minute," I said.

"All right." She hardly glanced at me; she yawned again

and wandered off toward the bedroom, stretching her entire body, arms above her head.

I walked across the courtyard and around the corner to the building's trash container. As I lifted the can and swung it over the side, something rustled through the garbage. Too loud for a cockroach. A mouse probably. I put the can down and stood motionless. Somewhere a few houses away a dog began to bark. The air was heavy with the smells of decaying fruit and vegetables, the stench of litter from the Siamese in the apartment below me, even a faintly human odor a little like spoiled milk. I breathed it in until it filled my head and threatened to awake a queasy feeling inside my stomach. And the longer I stood there, the more powerful it seemed, the odor of spoilage and waste overwhelming everything else. I felt for a second as though I could not only smell it, I could almost taste the rich and rotting fruits, and feel their skins beneath my fingers.

Then the queasiness subsided, and in its place came a curious sense of invigoration. It was as if whatever residue of taste and smell and touch had built up inside me was now wiped clean, as if my senses had been purged altogether. I walked back across the courtyard, empty can swinging at my side. The dog had stopped barking and there was no sign of a soul anywhere. I heard the solitary drawn-out whistle of a freight train from the switching yard on the edge of town. For a moment I felt purely alone, apart from everyone, even a little exhilarated. The sky was unusually bright, and only a few stars blinked out of it, looking very near and very plain to me, not at all remote. At my back a light wavered on the horizon, and it took me a little while to realize that it was what was left of the Highlands fire. Farther away in the other direction appeared a more familiar pink-orange glow — the steel mills starting a run, spreading their vague sulfurous light over the entire western sky. I climbed up the stairs to my apartment and stood looking out over the balcony. The view was not as spectacular as that from the Fairchild terrace, but it would do for me. The neon lights of downtown Birmingham were straight ahead and a little below me, and on either edge of the horizon the steel mills and the old clubhouse flared with lights of their own, as if in some curious way they mirrored one another.

Finally I opened the door and went inside. I switched off the lamp in the kitchen, and the apartment was dark except for a narrow rectangle of light coming from the bedroom. Down the hallway, I nearly tripped over one of Cassie's high-heeled shoes. When I stepped into the bedroom, I saw clothes scattered about the floor, her evening gown wadded into a ball in one corner. She was leaning over the back of a chair wearing nothing but one of my long-sleeved shirts, her bare legs twisted up sharply beneath her and angling toward me. At first I couldn't make out the sound that was coming from her — her shoulders and back shook in small, tight, convulsive sobs. I called her name, but she didn't move. Then I went to her and put my hand on her shoulder, and still she sobbed unyieldingly. I must have stood like that for more than a minute, my arm hanging awkwardly, hand resting on her shoulder. Finally I asked, with a coldness that surprised myself, "Why are you crying?"

"Because," she sobbed.

"Because why?" I insisted.

"Because everything is so hateful," she said. "I don't believe people ever love one another; that's just a word they use when they mean something else."

"I don't know what you're talking about," I said with a slight edge to my voice. "What else?"

"Oh, I don't know what I'm talking about either," she said. "What difference does it make? What does it matter why I'm crying?" And she looked around defiantly at me. "I'm crying because of the fire, because everything lovely ends in sadness. Is that enough for you?"

"I thought you didn't believe in ghosts," I replied rather roughly.

"I don't," she shot back, "at least not in those you can see. I've got ghosts — and demons — you'll never lay eyes on."

I was standing above her with my hands on my hips. Suddenly she whirled on me with the strangest look. I couldn't tell if it was disdainful or accusing, filled with fury or desire. Perhaps it was all those. When she spoke, her voice had an indefinable quality to match the expression of her face. "Poor sweet Nick," she said. "The incurable romantic. It never occurred to you that I might be a romantic, too, did it? Don't you know what the most romantic thing in the world is? Don't you know the truest purest act of love there can be?" She had stood up and was walking restlessly around the room, hugging her hands to her sides. Beneath the light cotton shirt her whole body trembled.

"One night," she said, "at Black Stone Manor, a night after a party like this, after the last guest had departed, the last guest had arisen and departed from my mother's bed." I watched her silently. "Oh, yes, we all know what goes on at Mama's little parties," she went on. "That's nothing new. Maybe you saw something tonight, maybe you didn't — I don't even want to know. If not, it wasn't for Mother's lack of trying.

"Well, one night after all that was over, I was upstairs undressing. I'd had a lot of champagne and I was a little high — not drunk, just tipsy. I remember I had taken off my onyx earrings, the ones I wear with the black sequined dress. And suddenly I stopped. I don't know why I stopped, but I did. Perhaps there is a kind of premonition that flashes through you without your even being aware of it. Do you believe that?

101

Anyway, I started down the staircase, and I could see a light coming from somewhere at the far end of the house. I knew it must be coming from the library. I walked toward it. I was barefoot, and as I walked through all those empty rooms I felt as if I were crossing miles of desert.

"When I came to the library I stopped just outside the door. Daddy was sitting far back in one of those big leather armchairs. His fingers were curled against his forehead, and there was a book on his lap, but he didn't seem to be reading. I moved in the doorway, and he looked up at me, a little startled but not exactly surprised.

" 'It's late,' I said to him. 'Aren't you going to bed?'

"He said, 'Not yet. I'm very tired. I believe I will just sit here for a few minutes.'

"I tiptoed across the room, almost shyly, I remember, as if he would scold me for being up so late. I was about to lean over and kiss him good night, but then I thought, If I do that, I will go upstairs to bed and he will be left here all alone.

"And so I sat down on his lap. When I was a little girl, I often used to sit on his lap, and he would read to me and then carry me up to bed." She was not trembling as before, but she said all this in a sort of singsong voice, as if she were a child reciting a poem. "I sat for a moment and looked at him — Mother always said we have the same way of staring at people. I reached my arms around his neck and I pulled his head down — you know how tall he is," she murmured absently, "and I kissed him. And then I felt his arms around me — they were hard powerful arms — and I knew at that instant that we both wanted exactly the same thing."

She stopped. And she looked at me as if she had just noticed I was there. "Does that horrify you? Do you think that's the most shocking thing you've ever heard?"

I didn't know what I felt — surprise, I guess, uneasiness perhaps — and the thought flashed through me that she would probably have *liked* me to think it was the most shocking thing I had ever heard. But I wasn't horrified. At that moment on this particular night, one of the damned out of Dante's *Inferno* could have staggered through the doorway behind us eating his own entrails and I don't believe I would have been truly horrified.

"Well, it wasn't horrible at all," she went on. "It was love." Maybe I stared when she said that because she repeated, "That's right: love. It was everything neither of us had ever had." She paused and took a step toward me. "I was sitting perfectly still, and he had his hands on my waist, and he moved them up until I could feel his fingers just beneath my breasts." Cassie was standing right in front of me now, and she took my hands and held them to her sides. She leaned her head back a little and looked at me from beneath half-closed eyelids. "I reached up and pushed the straps off my shoulders and the only thing keeping the dress from dropping right to my waist were Daddy's hands on me. He squeezed his fingers so tight against my chest that I thought I would die. Like this," she said. And she pressed my hands hard against her until I could feel my fingernails bite into her skin beneath the shirt. I didn't try to stop them. "At last I cried out. I didn't *want* to cry out," Cassie said as if pleading with me to believe her, "but I couldn't help it." There were tears in her eyes, of pain or anguish, I didn't know which. With some effort I wrenched my hands free of her sides. But she didn't appear to notice. "When Daddy heard me," she continued, "he stopped, he let go of me. And then I was half-naked right in front of him, sitting on his lap like some cheap little whore, I guess. And he looked at me with that look of wisdom he has." Now the tears rolled down her cheeks. "But I don't believe he was wise. Do you know what I think? I think he was a coward. I think Daddy's always been a coward. He was a coward when he married my mother, and he was a coward when he made every other important decision in his life."

She was crying, without sound, without movement, almost even without grief or sorrow, as if the action of her tears was all that was left to her. Finally I asked, "You don't think your father could have had any other reason?"

"What other reason," she said, with a slight sneer that reminded me of Timmy.

"I don't know," I replied, not fully convinced myself, "love maybe."

She looked at me out of red-rimmed eyes and bit her lower lip. What comes next is a little hard for me to understand or even admit to myself. I don't know what I had expected her to do. Perhaps break down completely into self-pitying tears. Or go flying out of my apartment (to whom? I wonder). She didn't do either of those things. Instead she pulled at the shirt, and it gave way with a high thin ripping sound. Ten seconds later it was on the floor, too, and she was standing naked in front of me, again with an expression on her face that reminded me of Timmy's — a sneer or a dare. I could see where my fingers had etched tiny red lines into the sides of her breasts. I reached out to pull her toward me, and I must have grabbed her along there because she gave a quick involuntary cry of pain. For just a second she pressed against me, and I kissed her, roughly, before she pulled away again. But she wouldn't let loose. She was leaning back, pushing me off and holding on to me at the same time. From then on we were engaged in a relentless and complex tug-of-war, as if there were a rope between us neither of us wanted to let go of. We moved around the room like that, my arms scratched and burning from wrist to elbow where she held to them. We knocked over a chair, and I banged hard into something with sharp edges — the dresser probably.

Finally, out of exhaustion maybe, she loosened her grip

and seemed to go limp, leaning toward me and then away from me in a gentle rocking motion. I had my hands clasped behind her, holding behind her buttocks, to keep her from sliding to the floor. She looked into my face and shook her head very slowly, smiling up at me like a too-knowing child. She wouldn't walk, wouldn't even acknowledge that her legs could support her. At last she put her hands on my shoulders, and I gathered her in my arms — lifting her from the back completely off the ground — and carried her awkwardly to the bed. When I put her down, she fell backward with her arms locked around my neck, pulling me down with her. She didn't have to pull hard. I fell over on top of her, on her soft belly damp where it veed together. I came inside her with my hands still clasped behind her. It was very quick and painfully sweet. And when it was over, I lay taut and still throbbing, our bodies so knotted together that I couldn't have moved if I had wanted to.

Almost as soon as it ended, Cassie fell into a deep trance-like sleep. But I stayed awake for a long while afterward. That night, for the first time, I knew I was no longer an outsider. I felt in a profound and frightening way that I had finally reached Cassie, and I had reached something in myself as well that I had never known existed. I even felt, now with all the perversity of a Fairchild, as if the act of love had been an act of faith, of allegiance, not just to Cassie but to her father, as if I had somehow committed incest by proxy.

All those thoughts burst and reeled through my mind like the fireworks at the Fairchild party. But before I could try to make sense of any of them, I drifted off on a whirling current of uneasy sleep, just as a thin gray mist of light began to filter through my curtains.

twelve

I slept as if I were circling on the outer edge of a whirlpool, so heavy with the weight of my own body that I could hardly shift my legs or even raise a hand, and I felt myself struggling to keep from being drawn down deeper into it. But when finally I was able to lift my head, I found that I didn't want to, and I tried to lie back down on the pillow. Everything I had been thinking, every sensation, came flooding back into consciousness, and I didn't believe I had been asleep for more than ten minutes. The same gray light was seeping through the curtains, only now I saw that it was brighter and fuller — morning light. And as I lay against the pillow — still too dazed to think and too exhausted to keep myself from it — I distinguished for the first time the sound that had actually awakened me. It became a firm steady knocking, not loud but insistent. With a faint sigh Cassie turned and buried her cheek further into the pillow. One of her legs stretched, then drew up again. The knocking stopped, but the silence sounded like no more than a pause. I reached for my watch. Nine-fifteen. Nine-fifteen on Saturday morning.

I got out of bed slowly, carefully, as if the bed really were moving beneath me, and tested my legs against the floor. In the bathroom I splashed water on my face and rinsed my mouth. The noise resumed, this time in brief energetic raps.

I put a robe on over my shorts, went to the living-room window, and peered through the venetian blinds. No clouds were distinguishable, no sky, nothing but a moving wall of iron-gray light that seemed to dissolve into drizzle of its own accord. On my balcony were two men. One was leaning over the railing with his back to me; the other was right up against the door, and all I could see of him was the side of a shoulder. Both of them wore dark suits, and the one in back carried a raincoat over his arm.

I opened the door. The man whose shoulder had faced me said in a polite impersonal voice, "Good morning, Mr. Phillips." Perhaps to make it official or perhaps only as a reflex action, he held out toward me in his hand a bright silver shield. He didn't have to. I recognized Sgt. Gann at once. The tall man behind him was Det. Newburn.

With some reflex action of my own, I kept the door only half-opened, my hand gripping the edge of it.

"We're looking for a young woman," Gann went on in the same expressionless tone. "Miss Cassandra Fairchild."

My hand tightened around the edge of the door. "What do you want with her?"

"Is she here?" he repeated patiently.

Before I could answer, I heard Cassie behind me. She had walked out into the hallway and stood squinting toward us, wearing only the man's oversized shirt she had slept in. I noticed that the right sleeve was torn at the shoulder. Newburn gawked and grinned sideways at me.

Cassie must have heard Gann call her name because she said, "Who is it? What do they want?" She rubbed her eyes and gazed curiously at the three of us through the haze of sleep that still enveloped her.

"Are you Cassandra Fairchild?" Gann asked.

She nodded at him with half-opened eyes, her lips parted slightly like a child who does not know whether to act surprised or petulant at being suddenly awakened. "Who are you?" she asked.

He held out his shield, although I don't believe she could have seen it clearly from that distance. "Police" — and he nodded in my direction, as if I were there to corroborate that. Then he said in a stiffly formal voice, "I am afraid I have to tell you that a woman whom we believe to be your mother was found dead this morning."

"What?" I looked at him like he had made some sort of ghastly mistake.

Cassie just stood there, her face unchanged. She made as if to shake some hair out of her eyes. "I don't understand," she said in a slow bewildered voice.

"I'm sorry, miss. You're the only one in the family we could get hold of. We'd like you to come with us and make a positive identification."

"Then you're not certain it's her," I put in quickly.

"Yes, ma'am," he said, addressing Cassie as if she'd spoken, "but we need proper identification."

Without saying a word, Cassie stared at all three of us, her whole body rigid, arms held stiffly at her sides, fingers spread apart. Then she began shaking her head violently, and she kept shaking it until I touched her arm.

"I'm coming with you," I told her. I looked toward Gann and he nodded.

She jerked her head up. Her face was pale and as blank as fine-grained marble. She looked at me, but not exactly as if she saw me, and her eyes seemed suddenly larger and much deeper.

"We can wait out here," Gann said, indicating the balcony. "We'll drive you to the —" He had, I knew, started to say "morgue," but he said instead, "to county hospital."

I still kept my hand on her arm. "Are you all right?" I asked.

She clutched her arms to her sides, then gazed down at the shirt she was clothed in as if she had no idea how she came to be wearing it. "I have to change clothes," she told me.

After Cassie had left the room, I asked Gann, "How can you be sure it's her mother?"

"Not much argument about that. The maid found her upstairs in the bedroom."

"What happened?"

His face formed a barely perceptible smile, more with his eyes than with his mouth, and he said, "Nothing natural, or we wouldn't be here."

"How did you know to come looking here, anyway?" I asked.

"We didn't know," Gann said. "One of the neighbors said she'd seen the girl at the party with a young man, and the Fairchilds' maid gave us your name."

When I went back to change clothes, Cassie was already dressed — in a skirt and a turtleneck sweater. She was leaning over the bedroom mirror putting on lipstick very carefully, as if a lot depended upon it. She didn't usually wear any, and it made her face look paler than ever.

Alabama, like most states, has a system of county coroners, and in Birmingham the morgue is in the basement of the county indigent hospital, a battered four-story brick building that must look very much as it did when it first opened its doors to the public in 1910. We drove around to the back and down a concrete ramp that fed into a pair of heavy swinging doors marked AUTHORIZED PERSONNEL ONLY. Inside, Gann asked us to wait and left us standing in the hallway with Newburn. Cassie fretted and glared around her as if impatient. I fidgeted and even Newburn looked a little uncomfortable.

No more than two minutes later, Gann reappeared with Dr. Nail, the assistant medical examiner. He spoke with a midwestern accent and had a briskly cheerful manner that seemed, under the circumstances, absurdly reassuring. He took us down a long hall, talking as we walked. "Now if you want to ask any questions," he told Cassie, "you go ahead." She didn't say anything and he went on, this time to Gann. "We haven't performed the autopsy yet, but I'm reasonably sure death was caused by asphyxiation. We believe a pillow was the mechanism."

We stopped in front of a dark green metal door and Dr. Nail said to me, "Normally only the next of kin are allowed in here, but if Miss Fairchild wishes it, we can make an exception."

Cassie nodded and said, "Yes, please."

He said, "Fine," and unlocked the door. We stepped into a small well-lit room with spotless white walls and a green tiled floor. It was nearly bare. Near the middle of the room a large round stainless-steel lamp was suspended from the ceiling and at the far end was another metal door with a small window. But none of that held my attention for very long. What I looked at — what all of us were looking at — was a dull metal table on rollers pushed up against the far wall beside the door. Without having to be told, we walked toward it. The medical examiner took hold of one end and rolled it out a few feet into the room. I knew that when a body is brought in for an autopsy the clothes are first removed and tagged separately. And for some reason I was painfully aware of the little peaks made by the bare toes beneath the rough white cloth. On one corner of the cloth I saw stenciled the words PROP/JEFFERSON COUNTY/AL.

"Are you all set?" Dr. Nail asked. Cassie nodded. He reached out and with a short, quick professional movement pulled the cloth from the face. Don't let anyone tell you that suffocating is not a horrible way to die. The mouth was twisted and the nose flattened to the right; the whole face in fact looked as if it had been shoved to one side by the force of what was done to it. The eyes protruded a little. And there were purplish blotches, like stains of some sort, especially around the lips.

Cassie stared for a full minute after I had looked away. At last she said, "That's Mother." The medical examiner flipped the sheet back up.

He led us back outside and offered Cassie a seat beside a gray metal desk in the corridor. "I need a few things for the death certificate," he explained. "Date of birth?"

"March twentieth," she said.

He waited a second, then prompted her, "The year?"

"Oh," she said. "I — I'm not certain. Nineteen thirty-seven, I think."

He nodded. "Place?"

"Macon, Georgia."

He asked one or two other questions. "That should do it. Sign here."

She fumbled with the paper before she found the right space, then bent low over it to sign her name.

Just as Cassie finished signing, the corridor door burst sharply open and Mr. Fairchild came in, a patrolman right behind him. He wore a tweed sport coat and worn corduroy pants. As soon as he saw us, he seemed to comprehend what had just taken place.

Cassie said, "Hello, Daddy." He went forward and hugged her. She stood expressionless while he kept his arms around her.

Sgt. Gann introduced himself.

"You should not have brought her down here," Mr. Fairchild said harshly.

"I'm sorry for that," Gann said. "We've been trying all morning to locate you."

"I was away from the house."

"The maid said she didn't think you'd slept there."

Mr. Fairchild looked at him for a second with an expression that seemed just short of contempt. "We had a party that lasted into the early morning," he said, "and I didn't feel sleepy. After a party that often happens to me. I sat up in the library for a time, and then I went for a drive. Driving relaxes me."

"Did you go by yourself?"

"No." He paused. "I picked up a friend."

"Anyone else see you?" Gann asked casually.

He thought about it. "Probably. We stopped at a truck stop for coffee — near Jefferson Point."

"That's about twenty-five miles," Gann said, half to himself. "When would that be?"

Mr. Fairchild shrugged. "It could have been six-thirty — seven o'clock. What difference does it make?" he said in a weary, exasperated voice. "What do you mean to suggest?"

"I don't mean to suggest anything, sir," Gann said in his polite, impersonal tone, "only that you come in and give us a statement as soon as it's convenient. And of course," he added, "we'll want to talk to your companion also."

Mr. Fairchild just nodded. He looked suddenly like a man who has traveled much farther than fifty miles. "I'm very tired," he said. "And I'd like to see my wife. Is she in there?"

Cassie left with her father; she said something about going to stay with relatives. I got a ride home in a patrol car. As I walked out, I saw Mike Stankey leaning against the doorway, joking easily with one of the patrolmen, toothpick bobbing from his mouth. We nodded at each other.

By the time I got home, it was half past ten. I didn't even

feel tired; I just felt as if I were a spectator watching someone else moving about in my body. I went in to work every other Saturday, and today I was due in a few hours. I stood for a long time under a hot throbbing shower, fixed a little breakfast, although I didn't eat any of it except the toast and coffee, and then got ready for work.

Saturday is a slow day. Much of the Sunday paper is made up in advance, and the deadline for the final is two hours earlier. Sometimes there is a football pool, even an occasional card game. That afternoon, however, seemed busier than usual. Over in the corner I saw Mike Stankey — a rare sight on a Saturday — crouched over the typewriter picking out keys with his index fingers.

So I suppose by that time everyone knew what had happened, and they probably knew, too, of at least a part of my involvement in it. Still, no one said anything. McDermott came in for a few hours every Saturday — to get away from his wife and three kids, most of us believed — and he didn't even look at me. He handed me back a story to rewrite and routed three obituaries my way. I played with the feature article for most of the afternoon. Sometime before five my phone rang. I looked up when I heard McDermott's voice, but he wasn't at his desk. He said, "Mr. Haroldson would like to see you in his office." Mr. Haroldson, the executive editor, actually ran the paper since the editor and publisher was now seventy-eight years old. I had spoken to Haroldson once in my life: on the day I started work, he delivered a nice welcoming speech of about ten words. He had been the city editor of a paper in Atlanta that won a Pulitzer; here he came and went according to his own mysterious ends, usually spending more time in Chamber of Commerce meetings than in the newsroom.

His door was half-opened, but I knocked anyway.

"Come in, Phillips," he said smoothly. The office was

plushly carpeted and there was actually a deer head with a nice rack on the wall. McDermott was leaning forward uncomfortably on the edge of an armchair.

"Sit down," Mr. Haroldson told me, indicating a chair that was the twin of McDermott's. "I got a phone call this afternoon from Captain Spain." Spain was chief of the homicide division. "It was a courtesy call. He wanted to tell me that one of my reporters was involved — at least peripherally — in a case under active investigation, and he wanted to assure himself that he would have our full cooperation. I told him of course that he would." He leaned back in his chair and put his hands behind his head. "Now, understand this: The only thing that might hinder you from cooperating fully would be if you were to learn something *as a reporter*" — he tapped his desk — "that you believe to be privileged."

"I understand that, sir."

"You may begin to find yourself in a delicate position — possibly you already have. I'm not concerned about your personal life. I'm concerned about maintaining the integrity of one of my reporters — and therefore of my entire newspaper," he emphasized deliberately, "and I'm concerned about our doing our job, reporting the news. You may have a special familiarity that would be helpful to us. On the other hand, your objectivity may be threatened and in that case you would be worth less than nothing. At the moment I believe Stankey is taking care of this?"

"He looked at McDermott and McDermott said, "Right."

"Now, before we go any further," he continued, leaning toward me, "I want to find out what you know, where you stand — so I'll know where the rest of us stand."

I told him all I knew was that Mrs. Fairchild had been killed. I had been to the party the night before with Cassie, and because the police had happened to locate Cassie at my apartment, I had gone with her to the morgue. Otherwise, I said, I knew nothing about the murder.

"Well," he said when I had finished, "you keep your wits about you. If there's anything McDermott or I can do, you let us know. It might even be good for your —" he hesitated — "your sense of perspective to get away for a bit." He turned to McDermott. "Have we done anything about those prison hearings in Montgomery next week?"

"Not anything I can't change."

"Perhaps it would be a good idea to send a police reporter down there, give us a new slant on things."

The rest of the evening was dull and slow. I ate a sandwich at my desk, then found myself watching the clock, although I was in no real hurry to get home. Hurlbut invited me along for a beer, but I was in no mood for that either. All day I had half expected Cassie to phone, if only to let me know where she was. Of course there was always the chance that I could reach her at Black Stone Manor. But I could not bring myself to disturb again so soon the unquiet air within that house.

I went out with a group of reporters who were on their way to Belle's. We parted company on the sidewalk, and I walked the block and a half to my car. It was still misting and the streets were nearly deserted, no sign that it was Saturday night. A few cars passed, headlights glistening. The only people I saw as I got into the car were three women standing like fixtures in front of the Milburn Hotel. They were unmistakable. All of them wore tight-fitting skirts, and two had beehive hairdos that were beginning to frizz. The third was younger and not so bad-looking.

Seeing them made me realize that I did not yet feel like going home. I stopped at a Waffle House and ordered scrambled eggs, sausage, and hash browns. I ate most of it and drank two cups of coffee. The food made me feel a little better. When at last I climbed the stairs to my apartment, it was after eleven o'clock, the first time I had been really alone since the police had come — no, since long before that, since before I had picked up Cassie for the party. And that was little more than twenty-four hours ago.

I began at last to remember how tired I was, although I felt a little wired from the coffee. I opened a beer and sat down on the sofa, stuporous and on edge at the same time. On television there was live wrestling from the municipal auditorium — the Masked Mauler versus a younger blond fellow named Kid Galahad. You would have thought the crowd would root for the young guy. But some perversity in them, or perhaps the unspoken knowledge that it was all a show and fixed in favor of the Kid, swung the audience over to the Mauler. I watched him lose in two out of three falls.

For the first time all day I allowed myself to think of Mrs. Fairchild. Whatever else she was last night, she had been very much alive and very human. I tried to call up the stark distorted mask of her that I had glimpsed this morning, but the transformation was so appalling that it seemed to baffle even my memory of it.

That was as far as I got. I was not yet able to contemplate Cassie or her father, or how they might be affected by any of this.

I remember thinking that I should turn the television off and go to bed. The next thing I knew, I was lying on top of the bed, gripping the bedspread as if it were hard earth and I were digging in for cover. I managed to crawl beneath the blanket before falling back asleep.

I slept hard. When I awoke, stiff and still in my clothes, the sun was shining through the curtains. I got up, showered quickly, and went out for a paper. Stankey's piece was the lead story and I skimmed it as I walked back to the apartment. It began:

Birmingham socialite Julia Fairchild was found dead early Saturday morning in an upstairs bedroom of her sprawling Buckingham Drive mansion. Baffled police say she was apparently murdered only a few hours after a lavish benefit party the Fairchilds hosted that was attended by prominent local guests and several foreign dignitaries.

The story went on to say the police believed she had been asphyxiated, but did not say how. And there was a lot more talk about the house and about the party the night before. Police had begun questioning the guests, the story said, but "as of late Saturday afternoon" they had no suspects. There was no picture of Mrs. Fairchild; instead they ran a large shot three columns wide of the wrought-iron gates at the bottom of the drive with the caption "Family withdraws behind locked gates after the tragedy." And there was no mention of Cassie except near the end, when the article listed the survivors and reported that the funeral would be Monday morning at eleven o'clock.

I fixed some coffee and read through the story two or three more times, until I had satisfied myself that it contained nothing new or unexpected.

Most of the rest of that day I stayed inside, watching a football game, playing with some notes I'd brought home weeks ago for a series I'd thought about. Late in the afternoon I picked up the phone and called the house and, as I had expected, got no answer. Around dinnertime I tried Melissa's, with the same result. I was debating whether to try to reach them at the funeral home when my phone rang.

"How are you?" I asked almost before Cassie could say a word.

"I'm all right,"she said. "I'm fine."

"I tried calling you at the house and there was no answer, no one at Melissa's either."

"We haven't been home all day," she answered quickly. "We stayed at Uncle Asa's, and today was such a rat race — the funeral home and the cemetery and trying to get ahold of all Mother's relatives. And that police detective had the nerve to call up here — Uncle Asa gave him hell."

The name sounded vaguely familiar. "Which uncle is that?"

"He's not really a relative," she explained. "He was grand-daddy's law partner. But he's always been like one of the family."

Asa Hammer, I thought, the old man I had met at the party. "I want to see you," I said.

"I'd like to see you, too." She paused. "I don't think I'd better tonight. Will you come tomorrow and stop by here after the funeral?"

"Sure," I said. I wanted to feel relieved when I hung up. But Cassie had sounded so good that she worried me a little; I guessed it was still a matter of time before what had happened would sink in.

Ten minutes later my phone rang again; it was Melissa this time.

"Sweet merciful heavens," were her very first words. "What a ghastly thing." Then she asked, "Are you all right, love?"

"Of course," I said. For some reason I was annoyed by the question.

"How is Cassie taking it?"

"She's okay — as far as I can tell."

"Yesterday morning must have been just horrible — I heard they dragged you down to the cold storage room."

"Who told you that?"

"I have my sources," she said. "You know, I spoke to Chapell. He's terribly upset." She stopped. "I believe I knew on Friday that something awful was going to happen. After that fire everyone's luck ran out. You're going to the funeral, I suppose?"

"Yes. It's tomorrow at eleven," I added, somewhat unnecessarily.

"I don't think I'll go," she said, sounding rather miserable. "I think it would be better if I didn't go. I'll see if there's something I can send. Give them my love, will you, Nick?"

I told her I would.

thirteen

*T*he funeral was at St. Alban's, the oldest and smallest Episcopal church in the city. The north-Alabama Episcopal diocese was essentially broad church — "bored church," Melissa called it. But the founding fathers of St. Alban's had fancied themselves linked, in spirit at least, to the Church of England, and they had constructed a richly elegant building to reflect that. Perhaps to emphasize its exclusive nature, the sanctuary was built to accommodate only a few hundred people, and when I arrived a little before eleven it was nearly filled. I recognized many of the same faces I had seen at the Fairchilds on Friday night, only now there was an air not exactly of shock but of dismayed surprise. They looked as if they had witnessed the entrance into the party of a malevolent stranger whose boorishness bordered on being obscene, and they could not understand why he had been allowed to stay. And back of their surprise was outrage, and behind that, fear.

Just past eleven the family walked in, straight up the center aisle to a pew at the front that had been tied off with black crepe. First came a couple I didn't know, then Mr. Fairchild, his shoulders stiffly squared as if holding himself erect with some effort. Next to him and about a half step back was Cassie, carrying herself almost primly, her hands clasped in front of her and eyes cast down. Timmy walked behind them with a kind of nonchalance that reminded me of the day he had swaggered out of his father's office. More strangers — Mrs. Fairchild's people, I supposed — straggled in after him.

After all that had come before, the service itself seemed no more than an interlude. There was no coffin — she had been cremated — and the minister's eulogy was the most tangible sign of death. The ritual grace had its intended effect; it made Mrs. Fairchild's death appear not as a singular horrifying event, but instead something of tragic dignity that mirrored the transience of human life. Perhaps for that reason it made me think, for the first time in years, of my father's funeral. A year after my mother left him, he had suffered his second heart attack, one too many. I remembered her at the funeral standing with a large taupe umbrella held by an anonymous hand above her, not crying but always seeming on the verge of it, while her new husband — a garment manufacturer from Fort Lauderdale — stood a little way off looking uncertain and ill at ease. And I remembered my own confusion of feelings: grief, which was in some bewildering way bound up with anger, and, added to that, astonishment, as though the anger had taken me by surprise.

I glanced now toward the family pew. Mr. Fairchild was gazing downward, frowning slightly, as if displeased with some particular aspect of the floor beneath his feet. Cassie sat with hands still folded, following the minister attentively. I wished I could know what she was thinking. But then I thought that perhaps she herself had no more than a vague idea of the emotions that warred within her. And I wished more than ever that I could comfort her.

I had grown used to the dimness inside the church, and when we stepped outside, the flat broad daylight surprised me. Asa Hammer's home was only a few minutes away, a graceful old brick house situated on the south side of Red

Mountain facing Shady Vale. A widower, he lived there by himself, but today there was already a line of cars in the drive when I arrived. Inside, the dining-room table was laden as if for a buffet. A maid walked soundlessly through the living room carrying a tray of fragile china cups and a silver coffeepot. At the end of the room was Mr. Fairchild, standing stiffly, his back to the fireplace. We shook hands, and I said what I suppose everyone must have said that day: I told him how sorry I was. He seemed in a distracted yet dignified way to be genuinely grieving, and I experienced a little resurgence of sympathy for him.

At that moment Cassie appeared at the other end of the room. She had evidently been upstairs changing; she wore a khaki skirt with a blue blouse, jade earrings, and fresh makeup that was blurred, as if she had put it on too quickly. Or perhaps it was simply not possible to mask the fatigue in her face. She greeted me with a light kiss on the cheek.

"How are you?" I asked. I told her I could only stay a minute, that I was due at work.

"I'm fine," she answered. "I'm starved. I haven't eaten a thing all day." She sounded almost chipper, except that the brightness in her voice seemed peculiarly remote.

We went into the dining room. Cassie fixed a large plate of fried chicken and potato salad, but I ate a good bit more of it than she did. I met Mrs. Fairchild's sister from Augusta and her husband, a slight man with a drooping tobacco-stained mustache. On my way out Cassie introduced me to Uncle Asa. He sat in a straight-backed chair near the door, his cane held stiffly in front of him. I had the feeling he remembered me from the party yet refrained from mentioning it out of a sense of delicacy. He didn't stand but we shook hands; his hand was thin and surprisingly strong.

At the front door I stopped and looked at Cassie. "Are you really all right?"

"Mmm-hmm," she said with a little shrug of her shoulders. She inclined her head forward so I could kiss her, but instead I reached out and touched the side of her cheek. She looked up, surprised, and for just a second her face softened as though she might laugh or cry. But she didn't do either.

"I'll call you later," I told her. "Good-bye."

"Bye."

The note in my typewriter at work read like this: "lt. o c harris cld, pls cl bk." Well, at least they had waited until after the funeral. By about an hour. Evidently the police had a rather economical sense of decency.

I dialed the number and a brisk woman's voice answered, "Robbery-Homicide."

I asked for Lt. Harris.

"Glad you called," he said in a voice that sounded calculated to invite a confidence. "I reckon you know what this is about. We think maybe you can help us out a little. No rush. Stop by when you get a chance."

"All right," I said. "I will."

"'Bout four o'clock this afternoon might be a real good time," he suggested.

"I'll be there," I said.

"That'll be fine."

When I walked in Harris was away from his desk. I sat down in a tiny railed-off area at the front of the detectives' room and waited. He appeared ten minutes later, giving me a near-conspiratorial grin and a handshake.

"Sorry I got hung up. Come on back," he said, putting a hand on my shoulder and guiding me between the desks. "You want some coffee?"

"No thanks." I wasn't used to that sort of hospitality.

"It'll be quieter in here." He ushered me into one of the

interrogation rooms around the corner. It was like the one downstairs in the jail except that the table in the middle was a dark brown with wavy lines in the Formica that were meant to approximate wood grain. And on it was a glass ashtray instead of a coffee can.

"Have a seat," Harris said as though we were in his own rather spartan living quarters. As soon as I had sat down, Sgt. Gann stepped in. He gave me the barest nod, then closed the door and flicked a switch that I knew turned on a red light outside above the door. When it is lit, it means an interrogation is in progress.

I shifted in my chair. "Do you plan to read me my rights?" I asked them.

Harris frowned. "We don't need that." And he reached up and flicked off the interrogation light. "All we want is a little cooperation. Why don't you sit down and get comfortable," he said to Gann.

"Now," he asked, turning back to me, "would it be fair to say you know the Fairchild family pretty well?"

"That depends," I answered.

"You must know the daughter pretty damn well," Gann put in.

I sat up. "What the hell kind of question is that?" I wasn't really so angry, I just didn't feel like being bullied.

"Simmer down," Harris said. "You don't need me to remind you we're conducting a murder investigation. There's a hell of a lot we don't know, and we're going to do our job the best way we know how. So let's just try to respect each other and leave personal feelings out of it, okay?"

I said that was okay by me.

"Why don't you start by telling us just how well you do know the family. How long have you known the girl" — he hesitated — "Cassie?"

"About a year," I said. I explained how we'd met. "We've

been seeing each other for several months. Friday night was one of the few times I saw Mrs. Fairchild."

"Isn't that a little unusual?" Harris said.

"Cassie and her mother don't — didn't — get along."

He accepted the explanation and went on. "What about the rest of the family?"

"Well, there's a brother, Timmy" — Harris nodded — "I've only met him once."

"What's the matter," Gann asked, "she don't get along with him either?"

"I have no idea, she never talks about him."

"How well do you know the husband — Mr. Fairchild?"

"That's a difficult question," I said. "If you mean did I see him often, the answer is yes. He liked to talk to me." I wondered to myself why I was speaking of Mr. Fairchild in the past tense.

"What did he talk about?"

"A lot of things, nothing in particular. Books, politics, history, poetry sometimes."

"Did he ever mention his family, his wife?"

I thought for a second. "Not that I remember."

"You ever hear anything about their marriage — from anyone?"

"Sure," I answered, "rumors. You always hear rumors about people like that."

"People like what?" Gann asked.

"Wealthy people, especially wealthy people who give lots of parties."

"Do you know a woman by the name of Melissa Hollingsworth?"

"Yes, I know her," I said evenly.

"We been told she's Fairchild's mistress."

The word struck me as oddly old-fashioned and I had to concentrate on what Harris meant by it. "I have no idea whether she is or not," I answered, careful not to say anything that I knew to be false.

"Have you ever seen them together?"

"Only on Friday night at the party. As far as I know, they're just friends."

"Purely platonic, huh?"

"I don't have any reason to think otherwise. Do you?" I asked, trying to reverse the roles for a second.

"Right now we got reasons to think just about anything we want," Gann answered.

I didn't say anything to that and the room was quiet momentarily.

"Let's talk about Mrs. Fairchild a little," Harris said, "since that's the reason we're here. You say you hardly knew her?"

"That's right."

"Did you know she had affairs? Know she ran around on her husband?"

"I told you, I heard quite a few rumors," I admitted, trying hard now not to tell an out-and-out lie.

"Well, suppose you tell us exactly what happened at that party from the minute you got there until the minute you left."

"All right." I began by describing the house and the crowd of guests. I told them about speaking to Mr. and Mrs. Fairchild and about seeing Melissa and meeting Jess, the bankruptcy judge. I told them about having an argument with Cassie over an old beau and about getting a little drunk. I described the fireworks. I even told them about the girl on the low stone wall doing the striptease. And I said the last thing I remembered before we'd left was standing on the terrace watching Highlands burn down. But I'd be damned if I was going to tell them that Cassie had led me up a secret passage and that I had stood hunched over in the darkness watching through a peephole while her mother sat naked on a bed being fondled by one of the guests.

While I was thinking this, Harris asked, a bit too casually, "Mizzuz Fairchild seem to be enjoying herself all right?"

"I suppose so," I said. "It was her party."

He gave a faint humorless laugh. "That's for damn sure. Did you know she spent a good part of it upstairs getting laid?"

"What?" I said it with something resembling disbelief, although I have never thought of myself as a good liar. And I don't fully believe I was lying then. No, I think that in some curious way I was actually shocked. What I had seen at the top of the passage that night had had the surrealistic quality of a fantastic dream; from where I had stood even the dimensions of the room were distorted. But the police reduced it to a flat vulgar reality. On top of that was my surprise that they had found it out at all. And I asked, genuinely incredulous, "How on earth do you know that?"

"Fellow volunteered the information," Harris said. "Young guy, lawyer in the firm the family did business with. He was damned nervous, too — nothing to worry about, though, we couldn't place him in the bedroom near the time of death. He said she was going to put in a good word for him." Harris laughed again, this time with a shade of humor. "We talked to a few other folks up there, learned a good bit, although some of it's ancient history."

I listened to all this silently, trying to betray neither too little emotion nor too much.

What he said next explained why he'd told me so much. "I'd have to say all that gave Mr. Fairchild a pretty good reason to want to see his wife dead. Wouldn't you?"

I don't know whether he believed that or just wanted to find out how I would react. But I could feel both of them looking at me. "No," I said, "I wouldn't."

"Huh," Harris grunted, as if he was mildly surprised. "Why not?"

"Because I don't believe he's capable of that kind of thing."

"That's not a reason," Harris pointed out.

"All right. It doesn't make any sense. You say she'd had affairs before, so why would this suddenly make him want to — see her dead?"

He looked blandly at me. "You tell me."

"He wouldn't," I said.

"Maybe he would, maybe he wouldn't. Somebody sure did." As he said this, he stood up. They were finished with me, for the time being at least. Harris thanked me and opened the door, assuring me that I had been "a great help."

"Anytime," I told him.

"Good. We'll keep that in mind."

He and Gann stood in the doorway while I walked on back through the detectives' room. When I got outside, I loosened my tie and discovered that, beneath my coat, I had been sweating.

fourteen

*I*t is only a ninety-mile drive south to Montgomery, but in some ways it is like entering another country. Outside Birmingham the last traces of the Appalachian foothills flatten out and for miles the land is red clay and scrub pine. Then it opens on either side into broad flat fertile vistas, broken only, as you go farther south, by rows of live oaks hung with Spanish moss. This is the Black Belt, named for the rich band of black earth that extends across the middle of Alabama and Georgia and Mississippi.

Here the Black Belt is watered by the Alabama River, which meanders, just outside Montgomery, in flat S-shaped curves through lush green fields rather like some life-giving river of the ancient world. Montgomery was the first capital of the Confederacy and it is the state capital, of course, and during parts of the year it fills with politicians like migrating birds. But at heart it is a small town, even a sort of country town. Rich in Birmingham means a big house on an acre lot inside Shady Vale. For less money you can live on a hundred acres outside Montgomery. In Birmingham business is conducted over lunch at the country club; in Montgomery, over shotguns on a quail shoot.

The day after my little chat with the Birmingham police, I put up at the Holiday Inn on Perry Street, about three blocks from Goat Hill, the felicitous name belonging to that piece of high ground where most of the state government buildings were erected. The Governor's Select Commission on Prison Reform was meeting in the capitol annex. The commission had been appointed partly to buy time — a federal judge had labeled one state prison "medieval at best" — and partly to convince the public that something was being done. Maybe something was. If that was the case, though, they probably had a lot of people fooled. During the four days I was there, they heard more than fifty witnesses, including three members of the state penal board who didn't agree on much of anything, an expert on "hereditary criminality" from Arkansas, and a Baptist minister who cited biblical texts in support of his stand against parole.

Still, I needed to get away for a few days, and the *Examiner* was picking up the check. Hal Irby, the paper's legislative reporter, took me along to a couple of cocktail parties. "This is where most of the real votes are counted," he said as we entered the ballroom of the Jeff Davis Hotel. "Looks like they got themselves a quorum this evenin'."

The party that night was being hosted by the Alabama Coalmen's Association. About half the state legislature was there, part of it sober. There were several other distinguished guests, including Miss Ruby, the aunt of ex-governor Big Jim Folsom, the football coach from the University of South Alabama (USA), and Miss Daytona International Speedway of 1978. I met a seventy-year-old "semiretired" state senator from Brewton who, when he discovered that I was just down from Birmingham, began asking me about the Fairchild case. "A few old men like me still remember Hoyt Fairchild," he said. That was Mr. Fairchild's father; he had been a state senator for a time before discovering that real power was to be had elsewhere.

"It happened at the house, didn't it?"

I told him yes.

"I went to a party at that house years ago." He paused. "She was a hell of a good-looking woman back then." After he said that, he turned his attention to Miss Daytona Speedway. And Irby took me off to meet the state highway commissioner "before he sobers up."

During the day when I wasn't at the hearings or working on a story, I walked around Goat Hill with the rest of the sightseers — schoolchildren shuffling single file, families on vacation who were not quite sure why they were there. We toured the Confederate Museum and the Jefferson Davis House and saw the Declaration of Statehood in the archives. Standing among the other tourists looking at grapeshot dug out of some battlefield or Davis's letters to Robert E. Lee, I began to get a curious sense not of our history but of our lack of it. For most of us the past seemed equally inaccessible whether as a source of strength or as an inducement to tragedy or folly. The museum said no more about who we were than if it had been a modern-day amusement park. In fact it probably said a good deal less.

On Saturday afternoon, after I had filed my last story, I wandered alone through the state capitol. It is a fine old building with white Alabama limestone facing, a splendid dome, and twin cantilevered spiral staircases. I spent a pleasant solitary hour loitering along its cool marbled corridors. In the west wing, an addition that dates from the 1880s, I came upon a portrait gallery containing, among the heavy gilt-framed governors and senators, a stark flat oil portrait of Frederick Ruston Chapell, Cassie's great-grandfather. He was twice lieutenant governor and probably would have become a U.S. senator except that he had run as a Democrat during Reconstruction. He looked young — perhaps it was made during his first term — and he had a lean, almost dashing face that was weighted only by sober heavy-lidded eyes. The artist had painted them so that whichever way you moved they seemed to follow you along the corridor.

I got back into Birmingham late Saturday night. Although I had been away for less than a week, as I drove through the downtown streets I had the sensation of a traveler who returns after a long voyage and is surprised and a little disappointed to find everything exactly as he had left it.

I was more than a little disappointed to find that the Fairchild murder was still front-page news. But I suppose I shouldn't have been surprised. The whole business, after all, was rich with the air of scandal, prime-time melodrama unfolding right at the kitchen door. Television reporters liked to square off before the gates of the house, look the camera in the eye, and sternly report that the police still had no leads whatsoever. One live call-in radio program — the kind that attracts lonely housewives and drunks — broadcast three separate confessions in the course of a week. Our paper, too, contributed its share to the sensationalism, including a page-two interview with Luther, the gardener. But for me the most disturbing thing of all was to hear absolute strangers talking about Mr. and Mrs. Fairchild — even Cassie and Timmy — as if they had lived next door to them all their lives. It was like witnessing an indecent act of a particularly insidious nature. And one morning in the Laundromat when I overheard two middle-aged women discussing theories put forth by the members of their respective church congregations, I lost control and actually told them to shut up and mind their own business. They gave me the kind of blank open-mouthed stares that they probably reserved for lunatics and atheists.

Cassie had moved out of Melissa's house and back up to Black Stone Manor. "I don't think Daddy should be all alone up there," she told me. The gates were kept locked to keep out reporters and curiosity seekers, and whenever I came, Cassie had to walk down and open them for me. I did not particularly like going there, and I didn't go often. In my waking dreams that house seemed a chill and lonely sort of bedlam, ruled by alien and distracted spirits. Moreover, I sensed that Cassie did not really want me to come. I do not think she wanted anyone there. It was as if she was trying to lock away that part of her life from all onlookers, strangers and friends alike. And I could not really blame her for it.

Still, I was uneasy over her. When we did see each other I felt as if we had a chaperone — some unseen presence hovering between us, watching all that we did. Or perhaps I should say I felt as if Cassie felt that way. There was something absolutely furtive about her. We did not make love often just then. But on one of the few occasions when we did — a Sunday afternoon in my apartment — she insisted on closing all the blinds, making the room as dark as possible. And she remained as hidden as she could beneath the bedcovers, watchful and alert the entire time, as if keeping guard over herself.

I did not see Mr. Fairchild at all. From what I gathered, he spent hours every day closeted with lawyers and accountants — Mrs. Fairchild's death generated business for just about everyone. But I did keep in touch with Melissa.

It would probably be more accurate to say she kept in touch with me. One afternoon I found her standing at my front door. "I was in the neighborhood, love, and I thought I'd stop by and say hello."

"I'm glad you did," I told her. It was the first time she'd ever been to my apartment.

"What a lovely view you have," she exclaimed leaning over the front porch.

I showed her around. She appeared delighted at the claw-footed bathtub and admired the glass doorknobs and some old wallpaper in the hallway, but she did all this in a slightly forced and distracted way. I made some coffee and we sat down in the living room. Melissa balanced the cup absently on her knee.

"Have you seen Chapell?" she asked me.

"Not since the funeral."

"Well, I haven't seen him at all. He won't see me, not now at least. He says he wants to keep me out of it, that he doesn't want to compromise my reputation." She gave a halfhearted laugh. "That's a hoot. What kind of reputation does he think I have left?" She sounded both miserable and resigned. "You know half the town believes he did it. And the other half — the ones who hated Julia more than they envied Chapell — they probably believe she was done in by an Abyssinian slave she kept locked away in her bedroom. Do you think he had anything to do with it?" she suddenly asked me. Before I could answer, she said, "Well, I know he didn't. Do you know why I know?"

I asked her why.

"Because he needed her. That's right, Julia made his life a living hell, and he needed it. Maybe he believed he needed to be punished for the death of his mother, I don't know. His psychiatrist might be able to tell you the answer to that one, although I doubt it. But I don't believe he ever had any intention of leaving Julia. She ran his life, she made him miserable, and he came running back for more every chance he got. I suppose he needed someone to blame his own unhappiness on, his own failures. Anyway, I know he couldn't have killed her; he had too much to lose. Of course," she said shaking her head, "I don't believe he could have done anything like that anyway."

We sat silently for a minute, both of us perhaps thinking over what Melissa had just said.

"It's sort of ironic," she continued. "She probably controls his life more now than when she was alive. Oh, well, I don't know why I'm defending him. I'm a suspect, too, you know." She said this as if she were just the tiniest bit proud of it. "Last week two of Birmingham's finest drove up to my door. It was kind of a hoot. One of them was wearing cowboy boots." Newburn, I thought. "Of course, they didn't say I was a suspect. They were very nice really, quite polite. But they asked an awful lot of questions about Julia and about Chapell and about me."

"That's just the way the police do things," I said. "They couldn't believe you had anything to do with it."

She shrugged. "Who knows what they believe; it's all such an unholy mess. And Cassie doesn't help matters much."

"What do you mean?"

Melissa shook her head. I couldn't get her to say anything else.

One day shortly after that I took Cassie to lunch. We went to a place called The Courtyard, a local institution run by two spinster ladies, which is about as close as Birmingham ever comes to the Old South. I don't know why I chose the place except perhaps that I thought it would be good for both of us to go somewhere different, someplace with no associations at all.

The weather was still warm and we took a table outside. Almost before we sat down I knew coming there had been a mistake. Four older women at a nearby table seemed to know Cassie; they smiled politely in our direction, then took to nodding and whispering among themselves once we were seated.

Cassie didn't turn around. But she was aware of being stared at. She looked at the place setting and fidgeted with her water glass, running her finger along the rim.

We were waited on by a striking young black woman dressed

like the rest of the waitresses in a green hoopskirt with a full yellow apron tied in a bow behind her back.

"What do you want?" I asked Cassie.

"Oh, I don't know." She glanced absently at the menu. "Just a bowl of she-crab soup, I guess." That was the house specialty, an old Charleston recipe.

I ordered the same thing and a club sandwich to go with it.

We didn't talk very much. The food arrived quickly and I discovered how hungry I was.

Cassie played with her spoon in the soup until she'd eaten about half of it. Then she said, "I want to leave."

"Right now?" I looked at what remained of my sandwich.

"Please," she said.

"All right." I got the waitress's attention and paid the check. As we stood up, we attracted more glances from the dowagers' table. I stared right back at the one closest until she gave a little forced smile and looked away.

"I'm sorry," Cassie said. "I know I'm not much fun just now. I don't like being in crowds where people can look at me."

"It's all right," I said. "We shouldn't have come here anyway."

When we reached Black Stone Manor, I pulled the car up at the bottom of the drive. We had left the gates closed but unlocked. As I pushed them open, I saw two children across the street watching us curiously. At the top of the drive I turned off the engine, leaving the keys in the ignition. We sat in the car. Finally Cassie turned to me and asked, uncertainly, "Would you like to come inside for a few minutes?"

I hesitated, not sure if she really wanted me.

"Come on," she said, "nobody's there except Viola."

I got out and we walked up. It was the kind of autumn

day — rare this far south — when the air is like crystal and you seem to see every vein in every leaf against a sky that is a deep clean blue.

Inside, the sunlight lit the house; tiny golden motes of dust rushed upward toward the ceiling out of my reach. We wandered through the downstairs, leisurely, as if we were making our way through a museum that we had happened to find empty of all other tourists on a lazy afternoon. Cassie walked around rather absently, from time to time pointing out something with the proprietarial air of a very frequent visitor.

As we sat on a wicker sofa in the sunroom, she said to me, "You've never really seen the upstairs, have you?"

"No," I answered. Try as I might I couldn't detect the slightest note of irony in her voice.

"Come on. It's about time I showed it to you."

There must have been a dozen bedrooms up there, richly appointed and filled with ponderous antique furniture, much of it looking as if it had not been disturbed in years. Even the closets had carved walnut doors and seemed as large as my own bedroom. I saw only one room that was sparsely furnished. Tucked away at the back of the house, it contained a brass single bed, an oak dresser, and a straight-backed chair. An Indian rug and a few piles of books were scattered about the floor. Without Cassie having to tell me, I knew it was the room her father occupied.

From there she took my hand and led me to the other end of the hall. "I think this is the most tasteful bedroom in the house," she said. "There's an old family story that Cousin Tallulah slept here every so often when she and my grandmother were little girls, but no one knows if it's true."

I let go of her hand and walked carefully around the room. I could tell Cassie was watching me. Finally I asked, "Why did you bring me in here?"

She shrugged. "Why shouldn't I?"

"The furniture's been rearranged," I said. "The bed was against that wall, wasn't it?"

She nodded.

I suppose that was why I didn't recognize it at first. That and the fact that it was smaller than it had appeared, and covered in rose wallpaper, rather lovely actually, which didn't show in the half-light. But there was no question — it was the same room.

I asked her again. "What are we doing here?"

"It's my own house. I can do as I please."

"Fine," I said, "but I don't have to stay."

"I *want* you to."

There was a curiously full note in her voice. I turned around just in time to see her, balancing with one hand against the bedpost, stepping out of her blue jeans.

"Cassie," I said in a warning tone. But already it was too late. She had pulled the shirt over her head and was sitting on the bed.

"I want you to make love to me."

I didn't say anything; I just looked at her.

"I want you to fuck me," she said deliberately, "right here in this bed."

She took off the little that was left of her clothing, and I half expected her to lie back in some sort of stagy seductive pose. Instead she reached a long tortoise-shelled comb from the dresser and sat there washed in the afternoon light, naked and unmindful of me, combing her hair. She pulled furiously at it in a way that was almost painful to watch, until it stood out in a fierce red-gold halo all around her head. Yet I couldn't *not* watch her; and I began to be aroused in spite of myself.

But I was determined not to let Cassie see it. "I'm going downstairs," I said evenly. "I'll wait for you there."

She was off the bed and at the doorway in front of me

before I got out. Standing erect with her arms tensed out from her sides, she looked like a statue of some pagan warrior goddess — splendid, defiant, and almost delirious. When she breathed I could feel her nipples brush against my shirt.

"What's the matter?" she asked. "Are you afraid?"

I looked resolutely beyond her into the wide empty hallway. Angry and obstinate and straining with excitement, I told her to get out of the way.

"You just make me," she said in a thick rhythmic whisper.

"All right. I will." I placed my hands stiffly on her hips and started to lift and swing her out of the doorway. But Cassie pulled me with her, and we moved out into the hall holding to each other like two children learning their first dance step. We stood still for a second, and I caught sight of our reflection in a full-length pier glass: Cassie fiercely naked and I looking clumsy and encumbered in all my clothes. At that moment I heard a noise downstairs, a sound that was both ominous and familiar, although I could not at first place it. Then I realized it was only a clock striking, and I relaxed a little. But it occurred to me that we were in no condition to greet anyone who might come up. Without letting go, we pulled each other back into the bedroom and I kicked the door shut. And after a moment we were no longer contending against one another, we were struggling to get to the same point. I got out of most of my clothes as we crossed the room to the bed. I sat down and Cassie stood above me, her head lifted and her arms pressed stiff against my chest. I reached my hand inside her legs, sliding my fingers back between her buttocks, then quickly forward all the way up inside of her. She gave a fine long shudder and pitched forward until she lay with her chest against mine. I entered her like that and lay still while she moved in sweet piercing circles above me. Then I heaved her over and pushed deeper inside her until her breath came in gasps from between her teeth. And for a

few minutes I became an equal partner with her in whatever
love or crime or outrage was perpetrated inside that bedroom.
And I thought, This is what Cassie has been after all along.

Afterward, as we lay side by side against each other and
love or outrage had subsided, I asked her, "What made you
do that?"

"I don't know," she said staring up at the ceiling. "I thought
you'd like it. I haven't been so good for you lately."

"That's not the only reason."

After a time she said, "I wanted to see what it would feel
like. I wanted to know if it would feel any different in this
room, in this bed."

"Well," I said, "did it?"

"My mother died in this bed," she went on in a faraway
voice. She did not seem fierce or defiant now. With her breasts
small and childlike and the concave hollow of her belly, she
looked as slight and delicate as a young girl.

"Cassie," I said as gently as I could, "sooner or later you've
got to stop thinking about it."

"I can't. I thought you understood that. I can never allow
myself to forget it. And I can't forgive them for it either."

"There's nobody to forgive," I said. "It's over, you have
to put it behind you."

"There's Daddy. And Melissa,"she added.

"What do you mean?"

"I told the police they were responsible for my mother's
death," she said dreamily.

I sat up. "You *what?*"

"I did," she insisted. "I told them. But I'm not sure they
believed me. I think they suspected I was holding something
back."

"What the hell are you talking about?" I demanded.

She closed her eyes and breathed slowly and deeply. "All
the time it was me."

"You don't know what you're saying."

"Yes, I do. I know exactly what I'm saying. I killed my mother. I killed her over and over again. We all did. And now it's done."

"That doesn't make any sense," I said, breathing an inward sigh of relief that it didn't.

"Of course it does," she answered reasonably. "It makes perfect sense. Even my psychiatrist says so. He says I killed her in my subconscious. But he says many times people do things like that, and I shouldn't confuse it with what happened in real life." She talked about herself as if she were describing someone else, a casual acquaintance.

"He's right. It's not your fault."

"But what did happen in real life?" she asked wonderingly. "Nobody knows, do they? And they'll probably never know."

"Sooner or later," I said, "the police will arrest someone."

"Yes. They'll arrest someone." She was silent for a time and then she asked the same question everyone else had been asking me lately: "Do you think Daddy did it?" Without waiting for an answer, she said gravely, "If he did, I would rather he did it for me than for Melissa. I think that would be finer, don't you?" And she looked toward me and giggled uncertainly, like a guilty child.

"Your father had nothing to do with it, Cassie."

"You don't know," she said stubbornly, drawing up her knees and clasping them to her chest. "You don't really know anything about it at all."

. And I lay back on the pillow and thought that she was right, I didn't really know anything about it.

So perhaps it was an anxiety born partly out of my ignorance that impelled me to call Melissa that evening. I asked if she had seen Cassie.

"She came by two days ago — to pick up some things. She barely spoke to me."

"I just wondered. I saw her today." I was silent, hoping she would volunteer more, but she didn't. "She wasn't in very good shape." I hesitated. "She said some pretty wild things about her mother's death."

"I've heard it all," Melissa said with a short bitter laugh. "Not from Cassie, not firsthand anyway. She's been spreading it all over town."

So that was what Melissa meant the other day.

"It makes me want to just strangle her." She laughed ruefully. "I suppose that's an unfortunate choice of words, but it makes me angry. And it makes me sad, too. I know how Cassie is; she's just putting herself in a hole. I wish we could do something."

"Like what?"

"I don't know. Now I can't even talk to Chapell about it. I finally broke down and called Henry Blair Stanton yesterday."

"Who is he?"

"Her psychiatrist — off and on. I've known him for years; his family had the big Tudor house behind ours." She laughed. "I've even put in a few hours on his couch myself — it's not really a couch, it's more of a recliner. Anyway, I told him I was worried about Cassie. And of course he gave me all that horseshit about patient confidentiality and ethics and all. And I said to him, 'For God's sake, Henry, I'm not asking you to break a sacred vow or to commit sodomy, I just want you to take me to lunch.' Well, he knew he didn't have any choice, and finally he said he would. Listen," she said, "why don't you come with us?"

I was doubtful, but she persisted, and in the end I agreed to meet them. They went to a downtown restaurant that did a big lunch business; it was packed by the time I got there.

They had arrived first and managed to secure a table. Henry Stanton was not what I expected. He was a tall slender man with graying hair and a suntanned face; he stood when Melissa introduced me and spoke with a pronounced southern accent.

"We've already ordered," Melissa said. "Otherwise they wouldn't let us hold the table." I asked for the vegetable plate, and the waitress brought a basket of fresh sweet rolls and corn sticks.

For the next thirty minutes we made small talk while we ate. After the waitress had cleared the dishes away and brought coffee, Melissa said, "All right, Henry, I'm not going to pussyfoot around anymore. I want to know about Cassie."

He half smiled. "Now, Melissa," he began.

"Don't try to sweet-talk me. I'm serious. She needs help, I know that without having to be told. And you can't talk to Chapell about it, can you?"

He looked hesitant. "Her father has been a little — inaccessible," he admitted. "The truth is I haven't seen much of Cassie in the past few weeks."

"Well, she's been acting like she's lost her mind," Melissa said, "and not making any secret of it either. She's hurting herself and the people close to her."

"Just who is it you're worried about, Melissa?"

"Damn it, Henry, I'm worried about all of us. I don't want to see Cassie ruin her life. Or anyone else's."

"She's a very confused young woman," Henry Stanton said deliberately, looking at his fingernails, "and frightened. That's natural considering what she's been through. And unfortunately it has only exacerbated certain strains already present." He looked at us. "Cassie holds everyone around her responsible for her mother's death — and herself most of all."

"But she can't really believe that, can she?" Melissa said.

"Maybe not rationally. But the psyche isn't a rational creature, and it devises ingenious ways of trying to protect itself.

Within Cassie there are powerful feelings contending against each other — hurt, guilt, remorse, jealousy, love — all confused and bound up together. And her way of dealing with them right now is to project them outside herself — into the light of day, you might call it — where they become a little less frightening and a little more manageable. And so she accuses the people she loves of murdering her mother."

"How nice for us," said Melissa. "What do you suggest we do?"

"Melissa," he said, shaking his head slowly, "the only thing anyone can do is stand by her. Don't desert her now; she needs all the friends she's got."

fifteen

*L*unch with Henry Blair Stanton was on Friday. Monday when I walked into work, rumors were flying about an arrest in the Fairchild case. I tried to pin them down, but all McDermott or anyone else knew was that Mike Stankey had heard something.

At five o'clock, just in time to make the first-edition deadline, Stankey walked in the door. He went to his typewriter and banged out three pages. I know because I counted them. I intercepted him on his way to the city desk.

"What's going on, Mike?"

He shook his head. "They want to make an arrest real bad. They're tired of reading about it in the papers and seeing themselves on TV. Spain wants to bring in the lady's husband. But he's not sure what he's got, and he's a little nervous about how much pull Fairchild has around town."

"What *has* he got?"

"I don't know," he said, "except this. Fairchild took a lie detector test and the results were inconclusive. He didn't exactly fail, but he didn't pass, either."

"That's not even admissible in court," I said.

"No, it isn't," he admitted. "But it's going to be the lead in tomorrow-morning's edition. I heard more, too, but it's all rumor — nothing I can say in print. Now if someone," he said, looking at me, "was to interview a member of the family —"

"Forget it," I said and walked away.

Later on my telephone rang. An unfamiliar woman's voice, courteous and businesslike, said, "Is this Mr. Phillips?"

"This is Nick Phillips."

The voice identified itself as that of Asa Hammer's secretary. "Mr. Hammer would like to see you at your earliest convenience," she said.

"What about?" I asked.

"I don't know the exact nature of the business. I believe it is a personal matter. Would ten o'clock tomorrow morning be agreeable?"

It would be agreeable.

Hammer, Glove, Fairchild occupies the thirty-eighth and thirty-ninth floors of the Alabama Trust Bank Building — not surprising considering that three of the partners, including Asa Hammer, are directors of the bank. The same names show up again and again on the boards of the major companies throughout the state. It is the twentieth century's corporate version of the old Bourbon aristocracy, the Black Belt landowners who used to run the state during the last century having traded miles of rich black earth for so many square feet of glass and concrete.

I arrived a few minutes early and told the pretty blond receptionist I had an appointment. She looked slightly surprised, but she asked me to sit down and offered to get me coffee. Maybe Asa Hammer didn't see many people, or maybe they all looked like company presidents.

At precisely ten o'clock a secretary emerged and showed me into a walnut-paneled office about the size of my apartment. It had a sweeping plum-colored carpet, overlaid with a rather simple Chinese rug. At one end an antique sofa and chairs were arranged as if in a living room; at the other end a massive carved desk stood in front of a wall of bronze-tinted glass. At first I thought the room was empty. Then I made out, seated behind the desk, looking even smaller and frailer than I had remembered, Asa Hammer.

He did not stand up — it looked as if it would have taken a great deal of effort for him to come around from behind that desk. Instead he inclined his head and shoulders toward me in a brief perfunctory gesture.

"It was very kind of you to come," he said. "Please sit down."

I looked around; the nearest chair was ten feet away.

"Perhaps you should pull the chair up. This desk is so dreadfully large it's difficult to talk over."

After I was seated across from him, I said, "Your secretary told me you wanted to discuss a personal matter."

"I'm an old man and I have come to believe that the only important things left in life are personal matters. As you see, I do very little work." He spread his thin hands, palms upward, across the glasslike surface of the empty desk. "I come in here every morning as I have for fifty-odd years, and my partners kindly allow me to continue using this office, although" — he lowered his voice, giving an air of confidentiality — "we are terribly short of office space and I happen to know they plan to convert this into three or four stuffy cubicles after I am gone. But I suppose," he said, leaning back, "no matter who you are, the only things that count for anything are personal matters. Would you agree with that, Mr. Phillips?"

"That depends."

"Upon what?"

"On what you're able to take for granted," I said.

"Unfortunately there is very little any of us can take for granted in this life — except of course the certainty of leaving it." He said this last with equanimity, almost indeed with satisfaction. I listened.

"Death is a terrible thing," he continued, "for the living, I mean. It places a burden on us which is both inescapable and impossible to bear. Julia's death was particularly tragic for those she left behind. It is disgraceful the ordeal that family has been made to endure."

He paused a moment and looked at me. "I am speaking frankly with you, Mr. Phillips. Otherwise I would not be speaking with you at all."

I gave a noncommittal nod.

"Julia baffled her husband. He never fully appreciated her, I'm afraid. Oh, I know she had her faults," he said, looking steadily at me, "so do we all. But in her own way Julia was a great lady. She had a strong sense of family honor. Whereas Chapell" — he made a shrugging gesture — "Chapell has never known whether to try to live down his family's name or to live up to it. Julia did not have that indecision. She didn't bring money, but she brought fine blood. And she appreciated the importance of it.

"The gravest threat to our society today lies in our own casual dissolution of the family, children being reared by perfect strangers. Someday the historians will chronicle the decline of our civilization by its divorce courts, its child-care centers, its welfare mothers.

"But that is the one thing that still sets the South apart. Even in Birmingham" — he motioned toward the downtown skyline behind him — "which is trying its damndest to rush after Atlanta and Houston, the family occupies a place of honor. We still have a sense of lineage." For a moment he sounded like someone discussing the question of succession in a European monarchy. "From the first, Julia understood that," he went on. "She believed in it, she protected it.

"In her own way, too, she venerated those children. She

had her problems with them, certainly, all parents do. Do you know what she told me not long ago? She said, 'My daughter is lost to me.' I told her that wasn't so, of course, but I am afraid she went to her grave believing it. I do not know what the trouble between them was — perhaps nothing more than the fact that they were both women. At any rate, Timmy was more important — sons always are. It is through them that we live on, if we live on at all."

He stopped talking, and I wondered if that was all he had gotten me up there to listen to. He had leaned back in the chair and closed his eyes, and I was looking at the pale translucent lids. For a second I imagined that I could glimpse what lay behind them — an iron-willed old man inhabiting a vast empty universe. While he was still leaning back with his eyes closed, he said in a soft, barely audible voice, "So you see . . . it is especially painful that her own child . . . should be a cause of so much grief."

I wasn't even sure I'd heard him right, and I waited for him to elaborate. But he became quiet again; he seemed in fact to have forgotten that I was there. Finally I broke the silence. "I don't know if I understand what you mean."

He brought his chair swiftly forward, and his eyes were suddenly open and alert. "I know you are reputed to be an intelligent young man, proficient in your work and trustworthy in your personal obligations."

For some reason I felt the hint of a chill pass through me as he said that.

"You will have guessed that I am speaking to you about Cassie. I do not speak merely out of professional interest or loyalty, but out of affection — affection for her, for her family, for her mother. I believe you share that?"

I nodded. To myself I wondered if he, too, in years past, had been a visitor in Cousin Tallulah's bedroom.

He was gazing intently at me. "This ordeal, this scandal

must not be permitted to continue. She must *stop* giving it encouragement." He paused to let that sink in. Then he asked, "May I count on you to use whatever influence you have to help put an end to it — to insure that everyone, living and dead, may rest in peace?"

I told him I wasn't sure how much influence I had. And I added, "I don't believe anyone will have much peace until the police find out who killed her."

He frowned for a second, as if I had broached something off-color. Then he said, "Thank you for coming, Mr. Phillips. I'll have the secretary show you out."

"There's no need for that," I said. But she appeared in the doorway a few seconds later. As I walked out he was leaning back in his chair again, like an old man about to nod off to sleep. Somehow I didn't believe it.

When I got in to work, I checked the morgue for the file on the Fairchild murder. I read through everything we had written; the only time Asa Hammer's name appeared was in connection with the law firm. So I asked Maynard Walsh. Walsh knows dirt about everybody in town; his nickname is "the garbage collector."

"Asa Hammer," Walsh said, "he used to be called 'the Pope.'"

"Why?"

"Because everybody who wanted to be governor — from Jim Folsom to George Wallace — had to get his blessing first. Why're you so interested?"

I told him I'd been thinking of doing a series on Birmingham civic leaders.

"You better start with Bull Connor," Walsh grunted.

I sat at my desk and mulled over what Asa Hammer had told me. Then I looked over the newspaper stories again.

Stankey had said he wanted to interview a member of the family. Well, there was one member of the family who hadn't been heard from at all — the one Asa Hammer had said was his mother's favorite.

First I had to find him. I was prepared to spend the afternoon tracking him down. Instead the listing was right there in the phone book: Timothy Ruston Fairchild, 808 13th Ave.

I told Walsh I was going out on an interview.

"Who you going to see, Asa Hammer?"

"Good guess," I said.

The address was on the east side of town in what was once a solidly middle-class neighborhood. Now it was up for grabs. Some of the old-timers were still there, slowly wearing out with their houses, honest God-fearing people who had learned to fear other things closer to home. In the early seventies, during the brief flowering of Birmingham's hippie movement, the area had become a haven for young runaways, united by the trinity of peace, love, and drugs. Now here, as in most places, only the drugs remained. One of the large Victorian houses had been turned into a methadone-maintenance clinic, and there was a local population of transients and addicts living within spitting distance of it. It was in this neighborhood that I came looking for Cassie's brother.

The house had been yellow once. Skirting two sides was a wide wooden porch sagging in the middle, a two-by-four propping up the roof. Above the door was a fanlight, also painted yellow and missing one pane. I rang the doorbell. From somewhere deep inside the house came the high-pitched barking of a small dog, then silence. I rang again. More barking. I held my finger steady on the bell; at last someone began unlatching the door. It was opened by a girl who looked to be about twenty years old, wearing faded cutoff jeans and a halter top. She had dirty-blond hair and a thin sharp-boned face. "What do you want?" she asked, watching me steadily through the badly patched screen door.

"I'm looking for Timothy Fairchild," I told her.

I may as well have said I was looking for Mick Jagger. She just stood there gazing at me out of flat blue eyes.

"Do you know him?" I asked. "Is this the right house?"

"What you want with Timmy? You don't look like no —" She stopped.

I didn't see any reason to say I was a reporter. Instead I told her, "I'm a friend of the family."

"That's about the funniest thing I ever heard, mister," she said. Maybe it was. Anyway, she began to laugh, and as she turned and walked back down the hall, the sound of her laughter echoed oddly through the house.

I put my hand on the screen door; it was latched. From the back a voice called, "What're you doing out there, Eva Jo?" Out of the long dark hallway a slender figure approached. I recognized Timmy, even though he wore a light-colored beard that hadn't completely grown in. And his face seemed older than when I had seen him last. Still, it had that characteristic look — the lower lip sticking out slightly, just as Cassie's did when she was brooding, the rest of the face seeming to draw back from something.

"Hello, Timmy," I said.

He looked at me, with more uncertainty than surprise. Then recognition, the familiar liquid smile spreading across his face. "It's Nick, isn't it? Cassie's beau," he added with a light mocking note.

"That's right," I said. "Can I come in? I'd like to talk to you."

"Sure," he grinned, unlatching the screen door. "You're practically one of the family. Eva Jo," he called to the girl, "c'mere and meet Cassie's beau." Eva Jo nodded to me from about ten feet down the hall where she had been standing the whole time.

"Shall we step back to the library," he said in the same mocking tone.

Most of the house looked vacant. In a room where Timmy shut the dog up, there was a small chest of drawers and a mattress on the floor. Otherwise I didn't see any furniture until we came to the back of the house. "Make yourself at home," Timmy said. I sat down on a worn Naugahyde sofa. Timmy sprawled across an overstuffed chair, dangling his legs over the side. The only new-looking piece of furniture was a Mediterranean-style console color TV against the wall facing the couch.

Eva Jo stood in the doorway, looking warily from one of us to the other. Timmy said offhandedly, without glancing up at her, "Why don't you go take a drive, darlin'. We got family business to discuss."

"Yeah," she said softly, "okay."

Timmy watched her walk away. "So how're you and Sis getting on?"

"I didn't come to talk about your sister."

"Just a social call, huh?"

"I want to ask you some questions about your mother."

"Hey, man," he said, "haven't you heard; my Mama's dead."

"Do you have any idea who would want to kill her?"

"Why would anyone want to kill Mama?" he asked, looking almost incredulous, as if I had just made the murder up.

"The police seem to have some suspicions about your father."

"The police," he said with a laugh. "Do they get paid to sit around and think up that stuff? They ought to be on TV."

"It's no joke."

"It ought to be. Daddy couldn't kill anybody — except maybe himself."

"Maybe they know something you don't."

"What the fuck do you mean?" he said angrily. "Who the fuck are you? Man, you ain't no friend of ours. I know who you are," Timmy went on. "Big-shot newspaper reporter. Going to get an exclusive interview. Well, why don't you interview Cassie? Yeah, that would make some hell of a story," he sneered. "Smear it across the front page."

I told him I wasn't interested in a story, I was interested in finding out what happened.

"Well, I don't know what happened. All I know she's dead. And nothing's going to bring her back. Nothing," he said to himself.

"I'm sorry."

"Yeah. The whole fucking world is sorry," Timmy said. "You think you can find your own way out? Or you want me to fucking ring for the butler?"

I walked out. When I stepped outside, I saw Eva Jo. She was sitting in the front seat of a rusty green Plymouth, its wheels jacked up on concrete blocks, the engine racing, hard rock booming from the radio.

sixteen

When I got back to the office, Walsh said McDermott had been looking for me. Before I could check my messages, he found me.

"How about doing a little newspaper work on our time," he said.

I said sure.

He handed me some old clippings and said, "There's some legwork here that ought to keep you busy for a couple of days." The assignment was one of those follow-up stories that nobody ever reads, an update on the unsolved murder of Fonda Trafford.

I drove out to Hueytown the next morning for the first time since that night back in early June. The area was probably better seen through the fitful glare of passing headlights. Viewed now in the broad flat daylight, it was an oppressively dreary landscape, neither rural nor urban. For miles there was a tangled wilderness of scrub pines, tin cans, and bits of rubbish, all nourished by the county landfill out of which they had grown. Beyond that, a limestone quarry and an abandoned strip-mine operation, looking like the surface of two moons, one newly scarred and the other long since inactive.

As I neared Hueytown itself, one sort of wilderness began to give way to another. I passed a trailer park. The teepee-shaped units of the Tomahawk Motel. The NASCAR King Kar Lot. Looming over everything was an amorphous mass of factory buildings, slag heaps, and settling pools — the Birmingham Division of U.S. Steel.

My first stop was a roadhouse called Popeye's, where the girl had worked as a waitress. It was empty except for a lone beer drinker in a cowboy hat and a kid working the pinball machine. The name Fonda Trafford didn't mean a thing to the waitress; she had only been there two weeks.

The cashier had been around long enough to watch lots of girls like Fonda come and go. "Sure, I remember her," she said. "She was prettier than the others." Nearby, the new waitress gave a little toss of her head and sashayed over toward the lone beer drinker. "What you asking about her now for?"

I told her I was writing a follow-up story. "How well did you know her?"

"She was different from the girls we usually get here — like Shera there. She acted like she didn't belong, like she deserved somethin' better." She laughed harshly. "I reckon she deserved better than what she got. You think they'll ever catch the one who done it?"

"Maybe." I asked who her friends were.

The woman shook her head. "She kept to herself a lot. You know, the others would talk about their fellas. But not Fonda. She was a tight-lipped little thing. It was almost like she was hiding something."

I thanked her and drove on into Bessemer. I talked to the sales clerk at Little Nothings, where police had traced the underclothing they eventually identified the dead girl by. "She came in a few times," the clerk said. "I recognized her picture in the paper. If I'd had her looks, I'da found me a ticket out of here by now."

I talked to a few other people who knew her. The main thing I discovered was that the cashier was right: Fonda did keep to herself.

The sales clerk at Little Nothings had given me a line on the girl who had shared a trailer with Fonda Trafford, and I spent the next morning tracking her down.

The first place I tried was a Bessemer auto-supply house. She hadn't worked there in six months, and the manager didn't know where she'd gone. But one of the customers, who had come in to get a rebuilt generator for his Ford truck, said, "You looking for Darnelle, go on down to the Zayre out the Bessemer superhighway. I seen her in there last week."

I found Darnelle Dawson behind the customer-service desk. She was a pretty girl who would have been prettier except that she had a bad complexion. She looked at me as if she had become accustomed to looking right through every person who stepped up to that desk. When I told her what I wanted, her mouth set into a hard thin line.

"Listen," she said in a husky voice, "that was a long time ago. That was a whole 'nother life. I'm getting married in three weeks. My boyfriend sells cars; he does real good. See." She held out her finger. "Genuine diamond. I don't even understand what you're doing here."

I said I just wanted some background information. I told her anything she could remember would help.

Darnelle said, "I didn't stay around there much, you know. I was over at my boyfriend's mostly. You think I wanted to live in a trailer?"

I asked if Fonda had a boyfriend.

"A lot of guys asked her out. I don't guess you ever saw her" — I shook my head — "she was real pretty. Fellas were always calling her up. She usually turned them down. I remember a guy called her at least three times in one week. She wouldn't give him the time of day."

"Why wouldn't she go out with anybody?"

"I don't know. Her daddy was so crazy, maybe she thought all men were like that."

"What was crazy about him?"

"He used to call her up, preaching at her over the phone about hell and sins of the flesh and all. If it'd been my daddy, I'd of turned into a whore just to spite him."

"But not Fonda," I said.

Darnelle pressed her lips together again, and gave me a hard stare. "Look, Fonda was my friend, okay? It was horrible what happened to her. But it happened, there's nothing left to say. I wish you'd just leave now, okay? I'm gettin' married in three weeks."

I said, "Okay," and drove back to town. As I passed the NASCAR King Kar Lot, I wondered if Darnelle's husband-to-be worked there.

When I got back to the office, I sat down to the story. It didn't want to come, but finally I turned out a few hashed-over paragraphs.

Almost five months later, Birmingham police are as baffled as ever by the brutal murder of a young Hueytown woman. Fonda Lyn Trafford's nearly nude body was discovered beside a deserted road by a Hueytown policeman on June 6.

The victim was shot twice, in the chest and abdomen. But authorities believe she died as the result of a beating she received before she was shot.

Soon after the killing, police brought a suspect in for questioning. However, he was released two days later for lack of evidence.

Miss Trafford, 19, was the daughter of a Luverne Baptist minister. She had lived in the Birmingham area for less than a year and worked as a waitress.

Friends say the attractive blond kept to herself but was well liked. They can offer no explanation for the killing.

"What happened to Fonda is bad enough," says a friend who asked that her name not be used. "But not knowing who did it, God, that scares me to death."

Police say the investigation is continuing, but they have refused any other comment on the case. In the meantime Fonda Trafford's murder remains as shrouded in mystery as the dark June night on which her body was found.

The story, along with a picture, ran the following Tuesday in a sidebar on page twenty-seven. The headline that went with it said: MONTHS AFTER SLAYING, POLICE STILL ASKING WHO, WHY?

That afternoon I got a phone call. At first I thought the caller was just another bored housewife wanting to talk over a murder story that had given her the only thrill she would get all week. But there was something unusual about the voice. I couldn't pinpoint any accent, but it was peculiarly exotic, as if the speaker had lived in a way that was foreign to the world around her.

"You are the man who wrote this morning's story about Fonda Trafford," she said.

It was a statement, not a question, but I answered anyway. "Yes, I wrote it."

"It is a long time since anyone has troubled himself about Fonda. I feel as if the person who wrote that story knew her."

"No. We never met."

"Of course not," she said. "Still, I wish you might know her."

"I'm afraid I don't understand."

"Fonda was a lovely child. I would like to tell you about her," she explained. "I would like you to be the one to hear."

"All right."

The woman gave me directions to a house between Hueytown and Bessemer, not far from the trailer Fonda Trafford had shared with Darnelle Dawson. Sitting on concrete blocks just back from the highway, the house was not much larger than a trailer itself. Nailed to a weeping willow in front of it was a wooden sign with an open hand painted in red. Beneath the hand in thick black letters was the word PALMIST.

I knocked and the door swung open immediately. "The people here call me Madame Anna," she said.

The room I stood in was of the same whitewashed pine planking from floor to ceiling. The floorboards were spaced a little too widely apart and drifting up through them was the faint dank smell of earth. I noticed a few unusual objects scattered about — some indeterminate wood carvings that might have been Indian or African and a rather ornate silver crucifix.

The most curious object of all was Madame Anna herself. She wore corduroy jeans and a rough cotton work shirt, but her hair was tied up in a dark red silk scarf giving her something of a Gypsy-like appearance. I would have guessed she was at least fifty, but her face was smooth and unwrinkled and it was impossible to judge her age exactly. She was Caucasian, I thought, although there was a slight sheen to her skin, as if she had some Cajun or even some Indian blood.

Without another word she led me to the back of the house, into a small sitting room that was heavily curtained and dimly lit.

"Sit down." She motioned to a large armchair. Not only the windows were draped but also the walls, giving the room a thick funereal atmosphere. I saw two more chairs, a table, and a daybed against one wall.

Madame Anna sat on a stool directly in front of me. She told me to hold out my palm. "The other one," she said when

I extended my left hand. She took my hand between both of hers, not looking at it, holding it between her two hands. She began moving her hands back and forth slowly — feeling from the tips of the fingers to the base of the palm, in the way a blind person might. It was an oddly sensual experience, intimate and yet impersonal at the same time.

Finally she looked down and began to study my hand. "You are a skeptical person," she said after a time. "You don't put much faith in what I am about to tell you."

"An occupational hazard," I said.

She ignored me and went back to the palm. "And yet," she said, "you have a deeply marked heart line. That shows a strong intuitive side, a feeling nature. Although the line is irregular — at times you fight against this in yourself. I believe you are the type who will fall in love in spite of himself — perhaps you already have — and yet you will love deeply and will persist in spite of pain and obstacles." She let my hand drop. "But you did not come here to learn about yourself."

"You said there were things you wanted me to hear. About Fonda Trafford."

She sat in silence for a moment. Then she began. "That child had a beautiful hand. Skin as smooth as honey. She came to me often — not as a client, you understand. Still, I would tell her what I saw in her palm. I told her she would live long and have a good life. She should have; it was written there." She paused. "The last time she came I saw more than her life. I saw two lives in her."

"What do you mean?"

"I didn't read that in her hand. I could see it in her face, her eyes."

I was still puzzled.

"She was going to have a baby," she said simply.

"A baby," I half said, half thought to myself.

"Her face shone with it," Madame Anna went on. "After I guessed, she took pleasure in telling me. She said it was a secret, that no one else knew."

"Did she tell you who the father was?"

"No. But I saw a glimpse of him."

"Where?"

"In here," she said, touching her temple. "I knew he was not like the boys out here; he had finer features. When I told that to Fonda, she was delighted. She was glad to be able to share her secret. She said they were going away to have the child."

"Why were they going away?"

"The boy was troubled — I don't know why. Frightened perhaps."

"When did she tell you this?"

"The last time I saw her — perhaps ten days before her death."

"Have you told the police any of it?"

"Oh, no," she said, as if such a thing were not even to be considered. "No. I make no business with the po-lice. If they ask, I would tell them. But they do not ask. They would think probably I am a crazy woman."

"Then why tell me?"

"Because," she said simply, "someone should know. And although you are skeptical, I believe you are trustworthy."

That made the second time in a week I'd been told that; it was beginning to worry me.

Madame Anna released my hand; the interview was over.

The next day I was at City Hall on other business. Harris was standing by the coffee machine talking football with Roy Jenkins. Jenkins had been a standout running back at Ohio State. After he made detective, some cynics said that for a black man to move up in the Birmingham Police Department, he needed to have gained at least a thousand yards a season. It didn't hurt that Jenkins was good at his job.

"Thought maybe you'd given up police work," Harris joked when he saw me. "I hope you didn't take things personally."

"No," I said. "I've been busy. The fact is I heard something you might be interested in."

"And what might that be?" Harris said, trying to scrape coffee whitener out of the bottom of a jar.

"It's about the Trafford case."

Harris put the jar down and looked up. Jenkins walked back to his desk.

"What did you hear?"

"I heard the girl was pregnant when she was killed."

"If that were true," Harris said in a measured voice, "we'd already know it."

"Do you already know it?"

He answered me with a question. "What made you start poking around in that?"

"It's been five months since the murder. We just thought it was time for an update. Maybe jostle somebody's memory."

"You guys kill me," Harris said. "You think just because we're not feeding you headlines, that nothing's going on. Where'd you go and hear a thing like that anyway?" he asked.

"Confidential source," I said. "Let's say I got it from a fortune teller."

"Unh," he grunted. "So you pick up a rumor from someone who don't want to come forward; that doesn't sound like much to me."

"It may be enough for a story."

Harris sighed. "I tell you what. You hold off for a little while. Don't go muddying the waters for us, I'll make sure you get a real story. As soon as it breaks."

"If I have to wait another five months, nobody'll be interested."

"You won't have to wait five months," Harris promised.

"How long?"

He shrugged. "Maybe any day now."

"I think you're sitting on something. You know more than you're telling me."

"If I didn't, I wouldn't be a cop, would I? I'd just be another half-assed newspaper reporter looking for something to write about."

seventeen

I had not seen Cassie in almost two weeks — since that turbulent afternoon in Cousin Tallulah's bedroom. Not that I hadn't tried. When I phoned she was out, and she didn't return my calls. But it was a pattern that was by now becoming familiar. I guessed she was, to use Melissa's phrase, "holing up." She would come to the surface when she was ready. In the meantime I could wait. Maybe I needed a little breathing room, too.

When Cassie finally did call, it was to invite me over for tea. She added, in a matter-of-fact voice that did not acknowledge her absence, "I hope you didn't take what I said the other day too seriously. Sometimes I talk too much."

"I've been trying to reach you," I said. "Where have you been?"

"I was away. I needed to get away for a little while. We thought it was best."

"What does that mean," I said, with a vehemence that surprised myself.

She hesitated. "I went to Pinehaven."

"Oh." That explained it. "Why didn't you tell me? How long were you there?"

"Only six days," she said. "I went in Wednesday a week ago."

"I see." Pinehaven was a private hospital. It specialized in the "discreet" treatment of alcoholism, drug abuse, and mental problems.

"It's not as bad as it sounds," she said breezily. "I think of it as a rest cure — like those spas in Europe where people went a hundred years ago to take the baths for their nerves or their livers or whatever it was that was troubling them. Of course, this wasn't so luxurious, and it didn't have such a high class of clientele. Still, they take care of you, they tell you what time to get up and what to eat and when to get your bath. There's something to be said for that."

"I suppose so," I said.

"I feel much better now," she said. "Besides I had to come home; I couldn't leave Daddy up here all alone."

After she hung up, I thought back over the past week and a half. Cassie had gone into the hospital the day after I had seen Asa Hammer. The coincidence was not reassuring.

The next afternoon I drove up to Black Stone Manor. Cassie opened the door to me and kissed me sedately on the cheek. We walked back through the house. "I thought we'd sit out on the terrace," she said. "What would you like?" A silver teapot was steeping on the table in the breakfast room. I said I'd prefer a beer.

"Daddy's sitting outside. Why don't you go keep him company. I'll bring it out."

I stepped through the french doors onto the terrace. No one else was in sight. I hadn't been out there since the night of the party. Even in the daylight it was an imposing prospect, but I found myself thinking about what a lot of lawn there was to keep up. In fact, all the grounds around the house seemed less well kept. There was a ragged edge to the line of boxwoods. The fishpond had been drained.

As I turned back toward the house, Mr. Fairchild materialized at the other end of the patio. We shook hands.

"Glad you came out, Nick," he said. "I've missed seeing you." I do not believe he even remembered my being at the funeral; he seemed under the impression that we had not met since the night of the party.

Cassie brought out a tray with tea, beer, and ginger ale.

We sat in wrought-iron chairs looking out over the wide expanse of empty lawn and tried to make conversation. "I've got to get that grass cut," Mr. Fairchild remarked twice. I didn't do much better. All I could think of to talk about were people who weren't there. Mrs. Fairchild. Melissa. Even Timmy. I began to suspect that Cassie had chosen to sit out there because such a vast empty space was necessary to contain all that had to remain unspoken. I wondered if I had been asked there to help break the silence or simply to be a witness to it. Until gradually I realized there was something more in their silence than embarrassment or grief. Something that passed back and forth in the intervals between Cassie and her father, while they kept it at bay without seeming to make a conscious effort — as if some unwelcome animal had taken up residence with them, and they had become accustomed every day to stepping warily around it. I could not make out its shape or color, but I knew what the animal was: it was fear.

Toward five o'clock it began to cool off, and Mr. Fairchild suggested we go inside. I said I had to be going. He seemed both relieved and sorry to see me go. Cassie didn't say anything. They both walked me to the door. "See you soon," I said to Cassie, more a question than anything else.

She nodded. I got in my car and watched them turn back inside the house.

*　　*　　*

Early the next morning Melissa, with her usual sense of timing, knocked on my front door. I was half-asleep and not particularly hospitable, but if she noticed she ignored it.

"Have you seen Chapell lately?" she demanded as she stepped inside.

I said I'd been up there the day before.

"He still won't let me see him." She walked past me and sat down. "I'm worried about him."

"Why?"

"I don't know," Melissa said. "Something's bothering him — something he's not telling me about."

"Did you know Cassie was in Pinehaven?" I asked.

Melissa had heard it. She didn't know whose idea the hospital was — not Henry Stanton's; he hadn't been consulted.

I told her about my talk with Asa Hammer. She listened silently. I asked if she knew why he was so interested.

She shook her head. "I know he's been a friend of the family for a long time. And of course he was Chapell's father's partner. There was some story about a quarrel between them," she said slowly. "He and Mr. Fairchild stopped speaking, I believe. But by then old Mr. Fairchild had stopped speaking to almost everyone, including Chapell. After he died, Asa Hammer was quite helpful with the estate."

"Cassie calls him Uncle Asa."

She nodded. "He's very old, eighty-five perhaps. But he's terribly powerful still. They say when Jimmy Carter was president, Asa Hammer used to pick up the phone in the morning and get Bert Lance out of bed. Be careful with him, Nick."

I said I would.

"There's something else, too." She hesitated.

"What is it?"

"I've seen her again," Melissa said in a soft voice.

She didn't mean Cassie. "Seen who?"

"The girl in the white dress. At the foot of the stairs."

It took me a minute. When I understood, it seemed like something that had happened ten years ago.

"I was at home on the sofa in the living room. I must have fallen asleep. Suddenly she was there. Exactly like she used to appear at Highlands before the fire. You remember," Melissa said. "One hand on the banister, about to step out onto the dance floor. Only this time something is different. This time I believe she sees me, too. She is looking at me — as though there is something I can do to help her. Suddenly the entire room lights up — as if someone has set off powder to snap an old-fashioned photograph. The flash blinds me and I close my eyes. When I open them, the room is on fire. I cannot believe how quickly everything is caught up in the flames. I can feel the heat as it moves toward me. The last thing I see is the staircase collapsing around her. When I woke up," she said, "I was clammy with sweat, and I couldn't stop crying. It makes me sad now to think about it."

"It's a sad dream," I said. "But it's only a dream."

"I believe in dreams," Melissa replied.

eighteen

*H*arris was true to his word. I was at home making dinner when the phone rang. I recognized his official voice. He said he had called my office, they told him it was my day off. The reason he was calling, he had made me a promise the other day and he was keeping it, if I felt like coming down.

I said thanks, I'd be there in a little while. I hung up, wishing he hadn't called me at home. It made me think of Gann and Newburn pushing themselves past me into the apartment. The place had not felt the same since.

Twenty minutes later I was in the detectives' room sitting across from Harris. "That business you asked about," he said, tapping a folder that lay on the desk between us. He opened it, read it over to himself, then read aloud: "Name Lonnie Wayne Skelton. Thirty-one years old. Last known address, One-seventeen Third Way, Bessemer. No regular employment. Warrant issued this day charging him with the murder of Fonda Lyn Trafford. Being held in Jefferson County jail in lieu of fifty thousand dollars bond." He closed the folder and put it inside his desk drawer. "That's the story," he said, leaning back in his chair.

"That's the first paragraph," I said. "How about the rest? Did he know her? Is he the one who got her pregnant?"

He shook his head. "We're still tying up the loose ends. I'll have to get back to you."

I went in to the *Examiner* and wrote it like that, stretching it to five paragraphs, making a few points for getting a story on my day off. After that I went out drinking with Hurlbut and Maynard Walsh.

The arrest of one unemployed Bessemer man for a killing nobody remembered did not stir a great deal of attention. It was barely mentioned on the six o'clock news. For the next two days I worked overtime on a story about fraud in the humanities department of a local junior college.

Lonnie Skelton got a little more interesting when Stankey heard there was a deal in the works. "Word says the DA is plea-bargaining him."

"What does Skelton have to bargain with?" I asked.

Stankey shrugged. "Search me."

I called Harris. He said, "That's out of my hands now he's in the county lockup. You want to know something, you talk to them."

The district attorney's office and the county holding facility occupy the top three floors of the Jefferson County Courthouse — an unfortunate design feature, since the jail plumbing has been known to back up and seep into the offices and courtrooms below. Fortunately, the legal machinery is experienced at handling such overflows.

Emory Fulford, the district attorney, was unavailable. I spoke to one of his assistants, who was less than helpful. He hadn't heard anything about a plea bargain until I walked in with it, he said, and he accused me of trying to manufacture a story.

I went upstairs, showed my press card to a khaki-uniformed sheriff's deputy, and asked if I could see Lonnie Skelton.

I waited. After twenty minutes, the deputy motioned for me to follow him. We went back past the holding cell — a dim cavernous room where sixty men sprawled on iron cots like lost souls in some institutional underworld. Beyond it were the interrogation rooms. Outside the last one, another sheriff's deputy was leaning against the wall. He opened the door and closed it behind me.

Harris had said Lonnie Skelton was thirty-one years old. He looked more like a dangerously overgrown bullyboy: too-large face with smooth, nearly hairless cheeks and pale lidless eyes, suggesting generations of inbreeding. Imbedded in the face, as a further sign of nature gone awry, was a tiny cherub's mouth.

Skelton was leaning forward, thick forearms resting on the table in front of him, his hands balled into heavy white-knuckled fists.

I sat down across from him.

He was working the fists, making the knuckles pop. "What you want with me?"

"I'm a reporter," I told him. "I'd like to ask you a few questions."

He eyed me suspiciously, as if he were about to catch me in a lie. "Who you with?"

I showed him my identification.

Skelton pointed toward the bare floor beside his chair. "Right there's your paper," he said. He leaned over and spat three times. "That's what I think of it. Now why'm I gon' talk to you?"

I didn't know. "Maybe you want someone to hear your side."

He sneered. "How dumb do you think I am? I ain't talking about this business here."

Maynard Walsh says interviewing some people is like getting a divorcée into bed. You're pretty sure she wants to, but you have to court her as if she doesn't. Lonnie Skelton took a lot of courting. But when I finally did get him to talk, he seemed to enjoy it.

He had been born in Bessemer, and I doubt if he had been more than fifty miles from there three times in his life. His father was a sheet-metal fabricator at the Connor Steel plant until it closed. His mother was "off somewhere in Louisiana."

"Do you have a girlfriend?"

"Nawh," he answered with what in some places might pass for a grin. "I got me a Jersey heifer."

"Did you know Fonda Trafford was pregnant?"

The semblance of a grin disappeared. He glared at me across the table.

"What's the matter?" I said. "That's a simple question."

"You *may* be a re*por*ter," he said deliberately, leaning heavily on each word, "but you *ain't squir*rel *shit* to *me*. You're *lucky* there's a *dep*ity out*side* that *door*."

I was wondering whether to push my luck and ask him again when the door burst open. I thought at first it was the deputy. Until I turned and saw a middle-aged man, solidly built, wearing a well-cut dark gray suit.

"What the hell's going on in here?" he demanded. "You." He looked at me. "Out." Then he said to Skelton, in a voice that could have frozen gasoline, "I thought I instructed you not to speak to anyone."

"Would you mind telling me who you are?" I asked. He could have been with the DA's office, except for the suit.

"I'm this man's attorney, and I'm telling you the interview is over."

"The interview's over when Mr. Skelton says it's over," I said, as if I thought he wanted to pour his heart out to me.

"You got anything else to say, Lonnie? Or you want to find a new lawyer?"

Skelton shook his head.

"It's over," the lawyer snapped at me.

On the way out I asked the deputy on duty who Skelton's lawyer was. He shuffled through some papers. "Name's Frank Kermany."

"Jesus." Kermany was one of the most expensive criminal lawyers in the state. "Who's paying his fee, the Legal-Aid Society?"

The deputy shrugged. "All I know, that's his lawyer's name."

When the city of Bessemer was founded in 1887, it was expected to rival Birmingham, lying as it does just to the west in the center of the mining and iron-making district. But the boom never materialized, the local land speculators went bankrupt, and today the broad avenues they laid out look peculiarly vacant. Bessemer's second peculiarity is political. Although the city lies within Jefferson County, it has its own courthouse distinct from the county seat in Birmingham. This was decreed by an act of the state legislature in 1926, in effect making Bessemer county seat to the mining camps and mill towns of west Jefferson County, an area that is chronically depressed and perpetually disenfranchised.

When I decided to try to satisfy my curiosity about Lonnie Skelton, the first person I talked to was Peg Mallory. The *Examiner* calls Peg its Bessemer courthouse correspondent, although for the past twenty-five years she has covered everything in Bessemer from politics to high-school football. She looks like your grandmother, and Walsh says she can interview the Bessemer police chief and hustle him at pool at the same time.

I told her about my interview with Skelton.

"What are you trying to find out?" she asked.

"Who he is. Why one of the most expensive criminal lawyers in the state is defending him."

She shook her head. "I'm afraid I can't help you much.

All I know about Skelton is that he did a little work next door."

"The police have him down as unemployed."

"It's not something you put on a résumé. He does a few jobs for Sonny Starnes."

"Sonny Starnes?"

"A local lawyer — unless he's been disbarred recently. They say Starnes does work for the redneck mafia. And I've heard he has a little loan business on the side. Just rumors, you understand."

"What did Skelton do for him?"

"Search me," she said. "Paralegal, you think?"

I called Starnes from a phone booth on the street and asked if I could have an appointment that afternoon. He said if I hurried on over, he'd see me in thirty minutes.

I ate a sandwich in the courthouse cafeteria, then walked next door. There was an empty storefront with an old Rexall sign hanging at a dangerous angle above the entrance. Starnes's office was one flight up and looked to occupy what there was of the second floor.

Starnes answered the door himself. He was a little shorter than I and a little heavier also. "Secretary's at lunch," he said. "Come on in."

I had expected Starnes to ask who had referred me to him, but he didn't. Maybe he was used to leaving such questions unanswered. Instead he got right down to business. "Okay," he said. "What do you need?"

I told him that I had inherited a little money from my father, which was true, and that I was thinking of buying some property for investment, which wasn't. I said I had my eye on an old house near here that could be divided into apartments. But I was worried about zoning problems as well as objections from the neighbors.

My legal problem didn't seem to excite him very much,

but it held his interest enough for him to ask where the house was. I gave him the name of a street. When I had finished, he said it sounded like there might be obstacles but he thought the problems could be worked out.

I asked if he had much experience at that sort of law.

Starnes laughed. "I've had a lot of experience at working out problems. Don't let the decor fool you," he said, waving around the room. "We're not fancy, but we've done work for people all over the country. I even handled a case once for a lawyer up in New York City, fellow by the name of Katzenbaum."

"No kidding."

"That's right," he said. "Some a' these fellas, even in Birmingham, they never been outside a boardroom. Between you and me, they'd be as lost in Bessemer as one of those high-priced New York Jews. You got to be a good ol' boy to get things done around here."

"I see." My father used to say the difference between a good ol' boy and a redneck is a good ol' boy will only hurt you if he has to.

"What business you in, Nick?"

"I'm a newspaper reporter."

Starnes grunted, as if the best use he'd found for newspapers was wrapping two-day-old fish.

"Sometimes it gets pretty interesting," I said.

"I bet."

"Like the story I'm working on now. About a girl who was murdered out this way last June. Her name was Fonda Trafford."

He was watching me a little more intently.

"Police just arrested a Bessemer man for the killing," I went on. "Maybe you know him, Lonnie Skelton."

Starnes took off his glasses and rubbed one eye as if he

were wiping away machine oil. "You're not looking to buy any property," he said. "Just what is it you're after?"

"Anything you can tell me about Lonnie Skelton."

"I don't like being lied to."

"Are you the one who hired Frank Kermany?"

Starnes stood up. "If you're not outa' here inside of thirty seconds, you won't be able to walk down those stairs."

"Thanks for the information," I said.

When I got back to the office, I called Harris. He wasn't in. I had written six obituaries before he returned my calls.

"I've got a few questions about Lonnie Skelton," I said.

"Couldn't the DA fill you in?"

"Could they tell me about Sonny Starnes?"

"Who?"

"Sonny Starnes," I repeated. "Lawyer and possible loan shark. And part-time employer of Lonnie Skelton."

"Yeah," Harris said. "I think I heard of him."

"Are you going to tell me about him? Or do I have to find out the hard way?"

"We know about Starnes," he said finally. "Off the record, he's been helpful to us — on more than one occasion."

"Including this one?"

"I'm not going to discuss a case under active investigation," said Harris, reverting to his official voice.

"So what am I supposed to make of it?" I said. "Starnes helps set Skelton up for you, then he goes out and hires Frank Kermany to defend him? That makes a lot of sense."

"Nobody set anybody up," Harris said shortly. End of conversation.

When I hung up the phone, McDermott told me to stop spending so much time on Skelton. "Nobody gives a shit," he said.

177

I said okay, I'd forget the whole business.

I did forget it. Until I got home from work and walked into my apartment.

I was going to put on a pair of shorts and run a mile or two before dinner, but something made me stop halfway down the hall. The bathroom still has some of the original fixtures; however, the old medicine cabinet above the sink had disappeared and been replaced by a large square mirror with a fluorescent light above it. What I saw, or rather what I didn't see, was the familiar reflection as I walked by.

For a split second I permitted myself to believe it was something the landlord might have done — the page of newsprint taped tightly across the bathroom mirror. It was completely covered. Except for one rectangular space of glass where part of the page had been cut out. Here deep grooves were gouged in an X across the glass. The landlord hadn't done that.

I stared at first, the way people stare at an automobile accident. Except it was like watching at the same time that you are trapped inside the wrecked car. My face in what remained of the mirror looked like a thick scarred mask of itself.

I took a step forward and examined the newsprint more closely. It was from the *Examiner* — Tuesday, November 8. I looked at it for a full thirty seconds before I figured out that the scarred section of mirror was where my story about Fonda Trafford's accused murderer should have been.

The full force of it hadn't hit me until I got an idea of what I was supposed to be afraid of. I sat down on the john, reached out and opened a drawer beneath the sink. I don't know what I was looking for. A dead animal perhaps. Instead there was a Gillette Trac II razor and a flattened tube of Crest toothpaste. The sight of the toothpaste made me feel a little sick. It seemed tainted beyond use.

Then I began to get angry. I made for the bedroom and dug an old baseball bat out of the closet. I did not really expect to find anyone; but I went from room to room, stepping behind doors, surprising the moths who haunted my closets, bat gripped like a bayonet in front of me.

All I turned up was an unstrung tennis racket I had misplaced months ago. No trace of anyone, no sign of entry, not even a scratch to show the door had been jimmied.

I took down the piece of newspaper, folded it carefully, and put it in the bottom drawer of my dresser beneath some shirts. The mirror looked oddly bare, the grooves standing out like fresh scars in a smooth young face.

So it was that easy. Someone, if he knew what he was doing, could walk into your apartment and do whatever he wanted.

But what did he want? To frighten me? Well, I was frightened, all right. And what was I supposed to do about it — call the police and report that someone had broken into my apartment and taped a newspaper across my shaving mirror? It would have been simpler if they had stolen my television. I could talk to someone at the paper, Walsh or Hurlbut. Yet somehow the thought of telling anyone seemed a little like betraying a trust. Because then I would have to answer questions. And I was not prepared to do that.

I made up my mind to be more careful. The next morning when I went out, I put a thin piece of tape across the doorjamb, something I had seen James Garner do on television. I didn't know if it worked, but it made me feel a little better.

The next few days were ordinary. No jimmied locks, no scarred mirrors. And I didn't think it had rattled me. Until I realized that I had begun to look around each night as I came home from work, and that I stiffened reflexively each time I opened my apartment door.

Cassie was coming over that weekend. And for some reason that, too, made me nervous. Maybe because I didn't know what I was getting into, and I didn't want to get her into it as well.

As usual Cassie surprised me. She was less preoccupied, less edgy, as if she had settled something with herself. The taut lines of her face had relaxed, and there was a hint of her old familiar expression — half quizzical and half amused. She wore jeans and a red gingham shirt, and I thought she looked terrific.

"What do you like best?" She asked me.

"I like the shirt best." I could tell before I unbuttoned it that she wasn't wearing anything underneath.

We went back to the bedroom and took each other's clothes off. It was the first time we had gone to bed since the afternoon in Cousin Tallulah's bedroom. Now we made love in our own sweet time, with a luxurious calm that made our earlier passion seem a high-school frenzy. Afterward we fell asleep. I dozed and awoke after a few minutes. Cassie was wrapped deeply in sleep, the blankets pulled tight around her. I got up and she didn't stir. But out of her sleep she murmured something, in one quick breath like a child's first speech, a whole sentence run together into one indecipherable word.

When I got back into bed, she turned over and opened her eyes. "That was nice," she said. "I'm hungry."

"Me too."

"You too what?" she asked with her quizzical-amused look.

"I feel nice and hungry."

"I bet you do."

Afterward we cooked bacon and scrambled eggs and sat on the sofa and watched the late movie on television. I was feeling comfortable and domestic.

I had lost track of the TV movie when Cassie said, "I read your story the other day."

"Which story?" I asked, a little surprised. She had never paid much attention to my work before.

"The story about that girl who was killed. The one with the curious name — Fonda — what was it?"

"Trafford," I said.

"Yes," she said. "Fonda Trafford." She was silent, but she seemed to be trying to make up her mind to say something else.

"What is it?"

"The thing is," she said, "I thought I'd seen that name before. I remember thinking that was a lovely name to be called by."

"Maybe you saw it in the newspapers."

"No." She shook her head. "It was somewhere else. I'm not sure. But I think I saw it in my mother's room."

I was listening.

"After Mother died, I helped Daddy go through her things. She saved practically everything. We threw out enough to fill an ordinary house. In her bedroom," she said slowly, "there was a mirror, one of those huge old gilt frame things, antique and terribly expensive, but a little vulgar, as if it belonged in a Victorian brothel. Anyway, Mother used to slide little scraps of paper under the frame — notes, telephone messages, and things. I always thought that was tacky, a venetian-glass mirror with bits of paper sticking out of it. I think I saw the name on one of those pieces of paper."

"Was anything else on it?"

She shrugged. "Some more writing, a phone number maybe, I don't know. I just remember the name because it seemed so unusual." She was silent for a moment. "Wouldn't it be odd," she went on to herself, "to think that Mother might have actually known that girl."

"Yes," I said, "it would be."

She looked up as if what I said surprised her. "I suppose

she could have been mixed up with one of Mother's projects. Maybe she was an artist of some sort."

"Maybe she was."

We didn't say anything else about it. And soon after that, Cassie yawned, said she was tired and needed to get back to the house. I walked her out to her car. We kissed good night. I had already started back up the steps when she rolled down her window and called after me, "Take care." Then she put the Honda in gear and drove away.

As I walked up the stairs, I said the two names out loud, "Mrs. Fairchild and Fonda Trafford," all in the same breath. Well, what did it signify? — you could put it down to sheer dumb coincidence. Only Cassie didn't believe that or she wouldn't have said anything. So you tell yourself that the past few months have been a kind of nightmare, and isn't this the way a nightmare unmistakably unfolds: frightening and wholly disconnected events coming together until they begin to seem ordinary and, finally even, inevitable?

nineteen

The next morning I drove out to Eastside. Sunday didn't look any different from a weekday here, the same barren streets, the same houses silent behind shuttered windows.

The green Plymouth hadn't moved, only a little more gone to rust. I rang the doorbell, three good long rings without getting an answer. This time, though, the door swung open when I pushed, and I stepped inside. Timmy was standing at the other end of the hallway, as if he had been there the whole time staring at the closed door. "What do you want?" He did not seem much surprised at seeing me.

"I want to talk, Timmy. Is your friend here?"

"Eva Jo's out walking the dog." He stood his ground at the end of the hall. "Who we gonna talk about this time?" he said in a little sneering tone. "Mama or Sis?"

"Neither one," I said. "I want you to tell me about Fonda Trafford."

Timmy stared blankly. "Who?" he said. "Fonda who?"

"You're going to have to tell someone; sooner or later the police will find out."

"Who?" he repeated moving toward me. "Find out what? Who was she?"

"She wasn't anybody," I said, "not to me. All I ever saw

of her was a still small shape on the ground beneath an army blanket."

"Jesus, man. Jesus," Timmy said. His expression didn't change. But his face turned pale, the small moon-shaped scars standing out white against his cheeks.

"It would help if you told me the truth, Timmy."

"Help who?" he asked. "Help who?"

"You did know her, didn't you?"

He stared right through me as if he were looking at someone coming through the front door.

"Was it your child she was going to have?"

He didn't answer.

"And your mother found out about it? Is that what happened?"

He squinted, concentrating harder on the door behind me. Then his face emptied of all expression and flashed a sudden quicksilver smile. "She didn't find out. That's not what happened at all," he said almost triumphantly. "I told her."

"You told her?" I said. "Why?"

"Why do you think? Hey, man, I was in trouble. I was scared. That's what I *do*. Mama told me not to worry. 'I won't have my grandchild born to a common low-class slut of a girl,'" he mimicked. "She didn't even know Fonda," he said softly.

"What happened then?"

He shook his head. "I don't know."

"You don't know who killed her?"

"Hey, get off my back, man," he said. "You think she died with my name on her lips?" A little of the swagger crept back into his voice. "I don't have to answer to you."

I heard the front door slam obligingly at that moment. Eva Jo came in with a half-breed terrier straining at the end of a leash.

She shot a look from Timmy to me. "We don't have to say

nothin' to him, Timmy," Eva Jo hissed. She jerked at the leash; the dog let out a whine that turned into a snarl.

I left, giving Eva Jo and the dog clearance, pulling the door tightly closed behind me.

It was my Sunday to work the late police beat. That meant sitting alone in the seventh-floor City Hall press room from nine-thirty to one AM. The building is empty that time of night, and I felt more isolated than usual. I had lots of time to think, and the more I thought, the more uncertain I became. I had come this far; I didn't know what to do next.

By the time I reached high school, my father had given away all his guns. But when I was younger, he had taken me hunting a few times, usually for deer. Once, in Sumter County, below Montgomery, we had been out almost all day without seeing anything. My father had followed the dogs and I was supposed to wait in the stand. But after a time I had started out on my own. It wasn't until I stumbled into a little creek that I realized I was lost. Alone, wet, and cold, I felt more lost than I ever had in my life; a feeling of terrifying uncertainty. My father had warned me that there might be other hunters nearby. I felt menaced now by everything that moved. Perhaps the best thing would have been to drop down and wait. But it was my first rifle, I wanted to get a shot off, and probably out of bravado more than anything else I pushed forward, following the creek bed. No more than five hundred yards upstream I startled a deer, a young buck with six or eight points. But he surprised me, too, and I hurried my shot, firing high. The noise led my father to me. He was angry but relieved, and, although he didn't say so, secretly proud of me for flushing the deer.

Now I felt the same temptation to drop down and make no movement at all. Only this time I had no one out there looking after me. No more safety in lying still than in plunging ahead.

Maybe it was bravado again, but it seemed the only thing I could do. My father would have understood that, and for the first time in years I wished that he were here to give his silent approval.

The next morning I called Asa Hammer's office. He was unavailable. "What is this in reference to?" the secretary asked.

"Just say that it's a personal matter," I told her.

A few minutes later she called back to tell me that for the present Mr. Lawton Diehl was handling Mr. Hammer's business. Mr. Diehl would be happy to see me at four-thirty if that was convenient.

Lawton Diehl's office was all chrome and smoked glass, no larger than an ordinary living room. When I walked in, he was standing in the middle of the room, watching me with eyes the color of the silver-gray carpet beneath his feet.

He nodded coolly at me. "I hope this needn't take up too much of our time, Mr. Phillips. I understand you've spoken to Timothy Fairchild. I hope you'll feel that you can speak freely with me. I'm the family's attorney."

I remembered then where I had seen him before — at the party the night Mrs. Fairchild was killed. Cassie had whispered, "He's Mama's lawyer."

I said, "You want me to tell you what Timmy told me?"

He dismissed that with a wave of his hand. "Timmy is an unstable young man; what he says is of little importance." He paused. "I'd like you to tell me what you think you know."

"I know about Fonda Trafford."

Diehl looked at me impassively. "Exactly who is she?"

"A young woman who was murdered about five months ago."

"And how should that be of interest to me?"

After that I started talking, perhaps more recklessly than I should have.

"Let me tell you a story, maybe you've heard it before," I said. "It's the story of a young man who is unstable and a bit weak-willed. He comes from a wealthy family, but he's been in trouble with drugs, he doesn't fit in, and he feels both dependent and resentful. He has a habit of getting involved with girls his family wouldn't approve of. He is more secure with girls like that, and maybe he also feels like he's asserting his independence.

"One day," I said, "he gets such a girl pregnant. It scares the hell out of him. He doesn't know what to do. Finally he goes to his mother for help. He hates himself for doing it, and he'd hate her more for it, but he does it anyway."

I went on to describe the boy's mother. "Her first concern might be protecting the family's reputation. But I think, too, that she would be jealous, jealous not so much of the girl herself, but of anything that might place her son beyond her control."

What would the mother do? I asked him. Try to buy the girl off, maybe even make threats? I told him that this girl was unusual. She was the daughter of a preacher, a man with a fanatical sense of right and wrong. She had run away from him, been on her own for a few years. And she believed she was in love with the boy. It was hard to predict just how a girl like that might react.

"One day," I concluded, "the problem disappears. The girl is killed. Five months later, to prove there is justice in the world, the police arrest someone, a local roughneck who is a little slow-witted. But he's got a crack lawyer, and he knows enough to keep his mouth shut."

When I had finished talking, Diehl said to me, "What are

you, Phillips? You're not a con man, are you? Are you one of those moral prigs who fancies himself motivated by higher principle?"

"Maybe I'm just a reporter looking for a story."

"Somehow I doubt that," he said. "Anyway there isn't any story here. This isn't news, it isn't even truth. All you have is a chain of suppositions, of hypotheses. Even if, as you say, the boy and his mother are in some way connected to this girl" — he waved his hand — "the law is not interested in conjecture about moral responsibility, it is interested in legal satisfaction. The police have their killer. That should be the end to it."

"It probably will be," I agreed.

"Then I don't quite see what you're getting at."

"Just this," I said. "I believe Fonda Trafford's killing and Mrs. Fairchild's murder are related."

"That," Diehl said, "is utterly ridiculous. It's preposterous."

"Maybe."

He frowned. "Do you have any — proof — to back this up."

"No," I told him. "Just more conjecture."

He had walked around behind his desk. "And what do you propose to do with this idiotic notion? Pass it on to the police?"

I shrugged. "I don't know." Before I had a chance to say anything else, there was a low tone, like that from a tuning fork. Diehl picked up the phone. He listened for a moment without saying a word. When he hung up, he looked at me. "Mr. Hammer thinks he should see you now."

Asa Hammer was seated behind the desk just as he had been the last time I saw him. That was weeks ago. Now the year was growing short, and evening deepened in the tinted window behind him. He made no movement to show that he was aware of my presence. The earth had rotated, but he might not have moved at all in the past two months. He simply appeared more remote against the darkening glass.

"This business has tired me out enormously," he said at last. "Why do you persist in trying to prolong it?"

"That's not what I'm trying to do," I said. I couldn't have told him what I was trying to do. But it didn't matter; he went on as if I hadn't spoken at all.

"Have you considered what effect this scandal — whether true or not — might have on the family?"

I told him I'd considered it.

"And you've considered the girl, Cassie? You must know how" — he hesitated — "delicate her emotional condition is. Have you thought about what the shock might do to her?"

"I believe she'd be better off knowing the truth."

"I see."

"Maybe you don't see. Cassie already suspects there's some connection between her family and that girl's death. She pointed me to it. Right now the truth probably couldn't be any worse than what she imagines."

Asa Hammer leaned back slightly toward the window. "So you believe that by proving her mother and her brother to be murderers, you will be rescuing her, that by damning them you will somehow save her from being swallowed up by the same damnation."

I had never put it to myself quite like that. But perhaps that was exactly what I believed. "Maybe," I said.

"That is taking a terrible risk. What if, instead of saving her, you cause her to be lost also?"

I didn't answer.

"In more than fifty years of practicing law," he went on, "I have learned two things: Whatever you think you know, it is but a small fraction of the truth of things. And whatever you do, the consequences of your action may be far different from what you imagine."

"And now you're going to tell me what I should do?"

"Stay out of it. You can only harm yourself and others."

"Is that a threat?" I asked.

His right hand lifted an inch or so off the desk. "I make no threats, Mr. Phillips. People who make threats usually lack the power to get what they want."

"So it's an order then?"

"Call it timely advice. Good day, Mr. Phillips. I do not think we need see each other again."

twenty

On Wednesday afternoon, barely forty-eight hours after I left Asa Hammer's office, McDermott walked back to my desk and casually let drop, "Cops finally found somebody to lay the Fairchild business on."

"You mean they've arrested someone?" I asked. "Who was it?"

He shrugged. "How should I know. Go over there and find out what's going on."

By the time I reached City Hall, the local TV crews were already camped out in the hallway outside the detectives' squad room, taking light readings and testing sound equipment. It took me fifteen minutes to chase down Harris. He was in a good mood. "Stick around," he said, "we're fixin' to have a party."

"How about filling me in?"

"Can't you wait for the show like the rest of 'em?" he said, motioning toward the hallway.

"What's the difference? We can't print it until tomorrow anyway."

He looked at me with something like amusement. "I forget, you got a personal involvement here. Almost family, ain't that right?"

"Almost," I said.

He nodded as if that satisfied him. Then he told me they'd gotten an anonymous phone tip to go to a northside rooming house where they would find some items stolen from the Fairchild house. The caller had given other information, too; Harris wouldn't say what, but it was evidently pretty persuasive. They obtained a search warrant last night, went to the house, and found Mrs. Fairchild's diamond choker and a watch in a room rented to one Wesley Waddell. When Waddell came in, they arrested him. He put up a fight, and they were able to charge him with resisting arrest along with possession of stolen property.

The police had a file on Waddell. He was a biker who had been thrown out of Satan's Disciples because he'd been on the wrong end of the drug business. "They'll push the stuff," Harris said, "but they don't like users, too unreliable." The investigation was continuing, but a preliminary lab test had this morning matched bits of hair taken from beneath Mrs. Fairchild's fingernails with hair samples from Waddell's arm. And that was enough to get a warrant charging him with murder.

"You don't think anyone else was involved?"

"Such as who?" Harris asked.

"I'm just asking."

"Stick around," he said again.

I stepped back out into the hall. One of the stations had sent down their co-anchor from the six-o'clock news. His crew practiced zooming in on him from different angles. The rest of us stood around or leaned against the wall and waited.

No one else seemed to notice Gann and Roy Jenkins enter the squad room through a side door. They walked stiffly, almost in lockstep, with Jenkins in the back, keeping his broad shoulders squared around. As they turned a corner I glimpsed a slender boyish figure sandwiched between them.

He ducked his head around one time, and I thought he might have seen me, too, but I wasn't sure.

I stood and watched the camera crew for another fifteen minutes. Then one of the uniforms stepped up to me and said quietly that I was wanted inside. Harris was waiting in front of the interrogation room, the red light above the door already lit. He told me Timothy Fairchild had requested that I be present while they talked to him. Harris didn't like the idea, but Timmy had insisted. I would be there only as a "relevant party" in a police investigation, he stipulated, not as a reporter.

Inside, Jenkins leaned against the wall, while Gann sat on the edge of the table. Timmy was sitting alone at one end, looking serious and subdued.

Harris did most of the talking. He was polite and official. He told Timmy that he was not being charged with anything, that he was only being asked to give information. He explained that they had arrested Waddell and were charging him with the murder of Timmy's mother. From what I pieced together after that, Waddell had had rambling, sometimes incoherent conversations with detectives in which he had made a number of claims. For instance, he had claimed that he was the illegitimate son of a high-ranking Columbian diplomat and had diplomatic immunity. He also claimed that he was helping Timmy recover some stolen property, which was why the jewelry was in his room.

They would like to know, Harris concluded pleasantly, why Waddell would say that. They wanted to know if Timmy knew Waddell and, if so, how.

Timmy said, to begin with, he had some drug problems and he was pretty sure the police already knew that. He said he knew who Waddell was and Waddell knew who he was because they had once been in the same local drug-rehab program. Waddell probably found out Timmy's family was wealthy. A lot of people did. And when they did, they usually tried to get something out of him, Timmy said. Maybe that was why Waddell had picked Timmy out.

Harris thanked Timmy, said he was being very forthcoming, and asked if he could get him something to drink. Timmy said he'd like a Coke. Gann left the room to get it, and Harris stood and talked with Jenkins. Timmy stood up, too, and I was standing next to him, close enough to touch him, and I looked him in the face.

In the next moment Lawton Diehl entered. He took in everything in one glance. Harris explained what I was doing there. Diehl said curtly that he would like me to leave. Timmy didn't say anything at all. After that Diehl took over.

I waited back outside with the other reporters for another forty-five minutes. Finally Harris walked out. With Diehl standing just to the side, he gave a brief professional account of Waddell's arrest. He indicated that Waddell had a prior criminal record. (I found out later that he had beaten a man to death for stealing his transistor radio. Perhaps because the victim was a junkie, Waddell had been convicted only of manslaughter and had served five years in the Georgia state prison at Valdosta.) Right now he was being held on charges of resisting arrest, possession of stolen property, and first-degree murder. Harris added that in order to further their investigation they had brought Timothy Fairchild down for questioning but that no charges had been filed against him. That was it, gentlemen, Harris said. Before it ended, the police had managed to parade Waddell past the cameras as they were transferring him to a cell.

After that the TV crews packed up their gear and left. One of the cameramen told me they were hoping to catch the finish of a stock car race. I had some time before my deadline, and I hung around a little while longer. Timmy and Lawton Diehl had vanished. Harris was still there, cleaning up his desk; I walked over and, without waiting for an invitation, sat down.

He looked at the clock and shook his head. "My wife'll have a fit when I say I been down here all night. I'd just as well come in drunk."

"You did all right today," I said. "Broke it wide open."

Harris looked at me. Then he said: "Police work's like anything else, you got to take what you get. You bust your ass for six months and go nowhere. Then you walk out the door one morning, and whatever it is you been looking for falls into your lap." He stopped. "Or sometimes you never find it." He watched me for a minute. "You get what you were looking for?"

"I got a story," I said. "I better go write it."

I got back to the *Examiner* about eleven — an hour before the final edition ran. "We're holding the front page," McDermott said as I walked through the door.

"I'll have it for you by midnight," I said. "Give me a little quiet until then."

Even though the city room was nearly deserted, I went into the managing editor's office and shut the door. This was the last time I would have the story all to myself, and I wanted to be alone and sort things out.

I worked at two stories that night. While I typed the one that would run on the front page the next morning, I tried in my own mind to make some sense of all that had happened. I didn't know everything, but I knew as much as anyone else, including the police. Part of what I didn't know then I discovered later. Or I guessed at. Asa Hammer had said you only knew a small fraction of the truth of things. The story I finally worked out for myself was more near to being true than anything I ever wrote in my life.

In fact, I believe I knew more about it than the police,

more than Lawton Diehl or Asa Hammer. Because I had been caught up for so long — body and soul — in the Fairchilds' tragedy, I felt as if I saw things from the inside out. Even when I had nothing more to go on than my own conjectures, they seemed more authentic than whatever signed statements the police might possess. In the end I believe I knew more even than Timmy himself.

Because by then I was almost certain that Timmy had planned it. Yet that wasn't right either. Because Mrs. Fairchild's death must have been less a plan than a convergence of possibilities. As if an astronomer, looking through a powerful but distorted telescope, could not only plot the movement of faraway stars but could actually set them in motion, calculating when they would come together, anticipating the cosmic explosion. So Timmy must have calculated.

First he had to goad or tempt Wesley Waddell into entering the house. Timmy must have known there was a good chance his mother would take a lover to that empty bedroom that night — as she had on so many other nights — the bedroom where long ago Mr. Fairchild's mother had slept and dressed for her beaux. He must have counted on her falling asleep there, too — with or without the lover — as she had so many times before. So when Timmy sent Waddell up that back staircase, when the secret panel swung open into the bedroom, she would still be there — lying beneath the white lace coverlet, just as her lover had left her. Perhaps Timmy even counted on her waking up, seeing the thick dark shape that didn't belong, and screaming. Counted on Waddell's grabbing the first thing handy — an old goose-down pillow, somewhat thin, in a white satin slipcase — just to shut her up at first. But once Waddell had pressed the pillow over Mrs. Fairchild's terrified face, he wouldn't be able to stop; his own blind fury and a longing for muscular release would take over.

So Timmy must have thought he could rely on Waddell.

He wasn't mistaken. He had kept the pillow over Mrs. Fairchild's face, had leaned his weight into it while her whole body bucked and kicked beneath the white lace coverlet like a drowning animal, and her hands clawed at the thick arms above her. (Besides matching the samples taken from Mrs. Fairchild's fingernails with the hair on Waddell's arms, the police found two-inch-long scars scooped out along his forearms.) He didn't flinch at the raw snapping sound as the cartilage of her nose was crushed, nor at the half-choked echo that followed when the hyoid bone in her neck splintered.

What did Waddell do when the legs stopped kicking and the body lay still, the hoarse barely human rattle beneath the pillow at last dead silent? Lift the pillow to make certain and let it fall back on top of her? Stare wildly around when he heard, in the sudden pounding silence, the creak of a stair or the shaking of a windowpane? Then, standing stark still and waiting, his eye might have been caught by the sparkle of the diamond choker catching light from the hallway. (According to the maid, Mrs. Fairchild always kept a lamp burning outside her door.) Whether it brought back to him his original purpose or whether it was pure impulse, he snatched it up — together with a diamond-and-emerald watch lying beside it on the dresser — and he ran. Not back the way he had come. He would move in a panic toward the door, just wanting to get out. Into the hallway, down the long sweeping marble staircase and then, perhaps guided by another shadowy impulse, he would run toward the back, not the front, of the house. There he found the door that led downstairs, unlocked it, and descended into the Norman Room. Perhaps some idea of his good luck flickered through his mind. At any rate he found himself in the same room he had broken into, knew exactly where he was, went through the same glass door, still standing open, and disappeared out into the night.

So it went, just as Timmy must have calculated. Yet to

say that he planned everything is to give Timmy both more and less than his due. It is to make him sound like a deliberate coldhearted murderer. And I don't mean to suggest that. Because I don't believe Timmy ever fully acknowledged to himself what he was doing. He must have known when his mother loved him that she loved him coldly for her own ends. Perhaps he even knew that for his mother all love, all affection, was an expression of power, power that she exercised jealously and absolutely, even over Timmy's girl and over his unborn child. And probably he had stored up more rage and hatred against her than he could measure.

Yet his mother's ruthlessness and his own hatred must have been too horrible for Timmy to face head on. It was this awful paradox that made Mrs. Fairchild's death possible; otherwise he could never have set it in motion. He did not tell himself that he intended her to be killed; he was planning a robbery, just as he had probably explained it to Waddell. In his own mind perhaps it would not even be that; it would be simply getting back a little of his own in the only way he knew. It would be, as Waddell had put it to the police, recovering stolen property.

And, if I was right, the most astonishing part was not Mrs. Fairchild's death itself; it was the inescapable correlation between the two murders. Wesley Waddell and Lonnie Skelton, one a drug addict and the other feebleminded, so much alike they could have come from the same family. The indifferent vast family of the Southern white lower class, to whom sudden unstudied brutality is as instinctive as chicken breeding.

But even more alike, more deeply akin, were Timmy and his mother. Timmy had learned from her better than either of them knew. And he had been true to her right up to the end. Each of them had set in motion an inevitable chain of violence — in deliberate and brutal ignorance of the ultimate consequence. The difference was that Mrs. Fairchild had never been confronted with the results of her action. But Timmy had. During that one moment in the interrogation room, just before Lawton Diehl entered, I cornered him. I whispered, "It was really you, wasn't it, Timmy?" At first he just stared back at me, with an expression both of horror and of vindication. Then the hint of a sneer flickered back across his face. And he answered with the same words he had said to me once before: "You're practically one of the family."

I had wanted to satisfy my sense of justice and to wash my hands of it at the same time. Instead I saw that I had given Timmy, out of the months of hiding and dissembling, his one moment of triumph. Maybe that was why he had wanted me to be there. I was Timmy's audience, and, more in some ways even than Wesley Waddell, I had become his accomplice.

twenty-one

I handed the story to McDermott and left without waiting for him to read it. When I stepped outside, the chimes of the Southland Insurance Building were playing "Dixie" — they do it twice a day, at noon and at midnight.

The streets were empty, and it didn't take long to drive home. As I got out of the car, I thought, At least now it's over. The police had their murderer. Waddell had done the killing, there wasn't much doubt about that. It was a lot simpler than trying to construct some elaborate conspiracy theory. It was simpler for me, too. I'd written my story. Maybe now I wouldn't have to put tape across my doorjamb anymore.

So when I heard someone behind me, I didn't pay any attention. Just as I reached the stairs, I turned around. It wasn't anyone who lived in the building. He was walking quickly, and I stepped aside to let him pass, but he stopped right in front of me. Suddenly he grabbed at me with a clumsy motion. It hadn't hit me yet to be afraid. But the feeling of his hand on my arm made me a little queasy. I tried to dodge away and swing out at the same time. My fist glanced off his neck — what there was of it — just beneath the ear. He stepped back, surprised. I swung again. But he was quicker than he looked. Before I knew I'd missed, he hit me in the stomach. "Stupid shitface," he said. "You try that again, I'll kill you." I wasn't going to try it again. I was doubled over, not trying to do anything but breathe.

He hit me some more, not as hard as the first but hard enough. I was on my knees, still doubled over, unable to raise my head. I looked at his shoes — they were the kind of work boots you get at a K mart. He moved as if in a crouch, circling me. Once I tried to stand. He stepped forward and kicked me sharply up under the ribs. "Stupid shitface," he said. "Sonny says you mind your own fucking business." He shifted his weight as if to kick me again.

At that moment I heard a door open and someone stepped outside. Thank God, I thought. Until I looked up and saw Cassie standing on my balcony. Don't come down, I prayed. And for the first time a cold emptying fear shot through me.

She saw me.

"Get back inside," I shouted. It came out as a roaring uneven groan.

In the next instant she was down the stairs and running toward us. He turned around just as she began screaming at him. "Bastard," she cried. "Son of a bitch. You bastard." He looked at her. She tried to hit him, and he caught both her fists in one hand and stood there watching, grinning at her. He had the same dull bullyboy grin as Lonnie Skelton. I thought suddenly of Fonda Trafford, saw her again curled helpless against the ground.

"Let go of her." I tried to get up. It was like climbing a staircase that wasn't there.

He hesitated for an instant. Then he shoved Cassie away and turned back toward me. I grabbed for his leg and tried to trip him up. He kicked again, his boot catching me under the chin, snapping my head back toward the ground. He stopped as if he was making up his mind what he wanted to do next. Someone pulling into a nearby driveway must have decided him. The car's headlights washed over us. After that all I remember was a sea of light threatening to float me away.

The next thing I knew, I was sitting, legs stretched out on the ground, Cassie kneeling beside me, holding on to me, still saying, "bastard, bastard," over and over, only now it was mixed up with her sobs. She asked if I wanted to go to the hospital. I shook my head, the blood dripped thickly from my nose.

It took a full twenty minutes for me to stand, cross the sidewalk, and climb the fifteen or so steps to my apartment. When we were inside and I was lying on the couch, Cassie picked up the phone. I could see her hand shaking.

"Who're you calling?" My jaw ached and the side of my cheek was bruised. When I talked, my face felt like a slab of broken cement.

"The police."

I shook my head. "No police."

"But that thug," she said, still shaking, "that hoodlum."

"No."

She stood with the receiver in her hand. "All right. But I'm going to call a doctor."

"Wait," I said. "See if Stacy — downstairs — will come up. It's simpler. And quicker," I added. The girl who lived beneath me was a fourth-year medical student. Cassie looked skeptical, but she went down.

Stacy was a tall, well-built girl who looked less like a doctor than she did a head nurse who wouldn't stand for any nonsense. When she walked in the door, she wore a curious expression that turned into pure openmouthed disbelief as soon as she laid eyes on me. After a brief and not totally convincing explanation of what had happened, she examined me pretty carefully. She went downstairs for some bandages and, with Cassie's help, taped my ribs.

"I don't think anything's broken," she said at last. "You're going to be real sore, but you'll probably be all right. Unless," she added cheerfully, "you have something like a ruptured spleen."

After she left, Cassie helped me undress and get cleaned up.

"I wasn't expecting you tonight," I told her. "I guess it was a lucky thing for me you were here."

She gave me a curious, unanswering look. Then she said, "I want you to tell me what's happening, Nick."

"You saw what happened."

"That's not what I mean, and you know it. All of it — your getting hurt tonight, that girl's murder — it's all got something to do with *us*, doesn't it?"

I didn't say anything, but she continued.

"My mother knew that girl who was murdered, didn't she?"

"I doubt if she ever met her," I said.

"But she knew who she was," she insisted.

"Yes."

"What about Timmy? Did he know her?"

I looked at her.

"He did, didn't he. He knows something about it and you don't want to say."

"He knew her."

"Does he know who murdered her?" she asked.

"The man who did it is in jail."

"That's right," she said, as if it had slipped her mind. "But that's not all, is it? Mother's mixed up in it somehow, isn't that what you think?"

"I think she may be."

"Yes," Cassie said slowly. "I know that. I suppose I've known for a long time — ever since I found that note. And Timmy," she persisted, "you think he did something terrible, too, don't you?"

"I think he did something," I said.

"Did he kill my mother?" she asked, her voice skating upward on an intake of breath.

What was I supposed to say to that? I shook my head. "The police arrested the man who killed your mother. It'll be in the papers tomorrow. That's why I was so late."

She looked at me for a second without comprehending. "You mean you — wrote the story?"

"Yes." I was suddenly uncomfortable.

"I see. Who is he?" she asked. "Who did they arrest?"

I shrugged. "He's an ex-con. A redneck. A drug addict. A psychopath. What difference does it make?"

"How did they catch him?"

"They found some of your mother's jewelry in his room."

She was silent for a moment. "You said he was a drug addict. Does he know Timmy?"

Now I felt cornered. "He says he was helping Timmy recover stolen property. He says that's how he got the idea. He's crazy. It's his word against Timmy's," I said.

"Oh," said Cassie. "So that's how it was."

She turned her back to me. I watched from the couch. She was hugging her arms to her sides and I could see her shoulders rise and fall as if she were breathing quickly. I went over to her and put my hands on her shoulders. She turned around. I tried to pull her to me. But she pushed me away, beating her fists against me, keeping me off.

"It's all right," I said.

She burst into angry broken sobs. "Bastard," she whispered through them fiercely. "You should have stayed out of it. Bastard, bastard," she repeated, just as she had out on the street, the same note of furious helplessness in her voice. And I realized that even then her anger had been aimed as much at me as at the man who beat me up.

"It's all right," I said again. "I'm sorry. It's all right."

She was still trying to push me away, but I held her fast, forcing her anger to exhaust itself against me. At last I felt her fists unclench, her body relax, and mine with it.

She took a deep breath and looked at me. "Poor Timmy," she said. "What's going to happen to him now?"

"I don't know," I said.

"Will he go to jail?"

"I don't know. Probably not."

She nodded. "Daddy used to say there was a curse on us. I didn't know what he meant. But I always thought it was me. I thought there was something horrible in me, and I was afraid to find out."

"There isn't anything horrible," I said. "It's all right."

She shivered. "I just want you to hold me for a little while. Just hold me."

I held her as tightly as I could.

twenty-two

*C*assie stayed with me most of the night, then left around daybreak to drive back to her father's house. I slept off and on, awaking for good about eight o'clock.

I lay in bed for a while, trying to find a comfortable position. At last I gave up. I took the bandages off my ribs and lowered myself painstakingly into the bathtub. After nearly an hour, the hot water began to bring me back to life, memory and pain returning to numbed muscle tissue. It took me another half hour to dry off and dress. Then I made some coffee. Finally I opened my front door. The morning paper was neatly folded on the doorstep.

It was the banner story — my first — with a five-column headline across the top of the page:

POLICE NAB SUSPECT IN FAIRCHILD MURDER
by Nick Phillips

Birmingham police yesterday charged Wesley Waddell, 27, with the murder of socialite Julia Fairchild, who was found brutally strangled in the bedroom of her Buckingham Drive mansion more than five months ago. Waddell's arrest came after police, acting on an anonymous tip, searched his room and discovered jewelry belonging to the dead woman, according to Police Lt. O. C. Harris.

Waddell was also charged with possession of stolen property and resisting arrest. The suspect has a long record of prior arrests and served five years in the Georgia state penitentiary for manslaughter.

No one except Waddell has been charged in the murder. However, the victim's son, Timothy Ruston Fairchild, 22, was questioned by police shortly after Waddell's arrest.

Informed sources say Waddell told police he was helping Fairchild recover some stolen property. Fairchild denied any such connection with Waddell.

Lawton Diehl, attorney for the Fairchild family, stated that his client "was in no way involved in his mother's tragic death."

I read through it twice, slowly. This morning it seemed even more contrived, more disconnected from the actuality, than it had last night. Even my byline looked out of place, as though I hadn't really written the story at all. The rest of it was continued to page three. When I opened up the newspaper, a plain white piece of notepaper slipped out and fluttered to the floor. I leaned down and picked it up. A few sentences were scrawled across it in a large childish hand:

Daddy was right all along. There is a curse on us. Don't feel bad, Nick. It isn't your fault. But I wish you hadn't been the one to write the story.

                                                              Cassie

I called Cassie at her father's and got a busy signal. I told the operator it was an emergency and asked her to interrupt. She said the phone was off the hook. There was no answer at Melissa's.

Something pulled at my ribs as I slid behind the wheel of the car. When I backed out of the driveway, the pain nearly took my breath away. I shot the seat forward as far as I could and drove slowly, hunched over the wheel like an old man, ignoring the horns of impatient drivers behind me, steering the car with both hands up the mountain toward Buckingham Drive.

Near the Fairchild house there was a car full of kids parked on the far side of the street, the engine running. When I slowed down, they pulled away with a squeal of rubber and a blast on the horn. I kept going, on past the house and around the corner, parking on a narrow street that came to a dead end near the top of the mountain.

I got out and walked across a neighboring lawn that was as wide as a golf course before I reached the Fairchild's driveway.

I rang the bell once. Waited. Rang it again. Finally the door swung slowly open.

Mr. Fairchild was standing in the doorway, wearing his customary tweed jacket, stooping forward a little, a book in his hand, eyes puffy as if he had been up all night reading it.

"You look awful," he said to me.

For a moment I'd forgotten about the bruises on my face.

"I'm looking for Cassie," I said. "I called a few minutes ago; they said your phone was off the hook."

"Yes," he said. "We're not taking calls this morning."

"Do you know where she is?"

"I haven't seen her since yesterday."

"Can I come in for a minute?" I said. "I'd like to talk to you."

We walked into the library. Mr. Fairchild closed the door behind him.

He sank heavily into a thick leather armchair, his hands on the armrests.

"Whoever the other fellow was, I hope he looks half as bad as you do," he said, with a short laugh.

"Compliments of Sonny Starnes," I said. "It was my fault — for not being more careful."

"Sometimes you have to take a beating," he said grimly. "Sometimes there's nothing else you can do."

"Is that supposed to be an apology or an explanation?"

"If you're looking for answers, you've come to the wrong place."

"I already know most of it," I told him. "I know about Timmy and Fonda Trafford."

208

He didn't say anything. He waited for me to continue.

"I think Asa Hammer is Timmy's natural father."

"Do you now?" Mr. Fairchild answered coolly. "My late wife used to repeat that to me on certain occasions. Is that all you came here to ascertain? Timmy's parentage?"

"I believe Asa Hammer kept Timmy out of jail. I'd like to know if you were part of it."

"You've still got an awful lot to learn, Nick."

"There are some things I hope I never learn."

"But you will. You'll learn them the hard way. As I did," he added.

"What? To sit and take it? To sit and watch while somebody you care about gets hurt, killed maybe?"

"Sometimes there's nothing else you can do," he repeated.

"I could go to the police," I said. "Or make it public."

He shook his head. "If you really wanted to do that, you wouldn't be sitting here talking to me now."

"Maybe not."

He smiled faintly. "You see, Nick. You're beginning to learn already."

I didn't want to learn anything. I wanted to grab him out of his chair and shake him. To shake somebody. Hit somebody. Asa Hammer maybe. Or Timmy. Or Mrs. Fairchild herself. Then I thought about Cassie. I remembered how I felt the night before when I lay on the ground and saw her leaning over the balcony above me. The sick fear that raced through me when she ran down the stairs. The only thing I was sure of was that I didn't want to lose her. Not now.

"Do you have any idea where Cassie could be?" I asked.

He shook his head. "I don't think she'll go far." Mr. Fairchild stood up. "We understand each other. I hope we're still friends, Nick. For Cassie's sake," he added. He held out his hand to me.

"What about Timmy? What's going to happen to him?"

"I'll see that he's taken care of," Mr. Fairchild said in a tone that held neither warmth nor bitterness. "Whatever the circumstances of his breeding, Timmy is still my son."

I shook hands with him. Then I walked out of the room.

The rest of the day I spent driving around town trying to find Cassie. I called Melissa's three times and drove by there twice. I went by Highland Park and a few other places we had frequented. I checked with Mr. Fairchild again and he said wearily that he still hadn't heard from her. Finally I drove up there once more to see for myself. But her car wasn't in the drive, and I didn't go in. For some reason I drove along Buckingham, past the houses, where the road became one lane, following the path of an old mining road along the edge of the mountain. It was almost dusk and the city that spread out below me was growing more and more indistinct, as if at any moment it would revert to the dark atavistic valley the Indians once knew.

Here the mountain became more rugged, road threatening to turn into trail in the next instant. The area was too steep for development, but the city park board had turned a narrow strip of land into a scenic overlook. There was a marker and a cannon — Civil War vintage — pointing out over the city. The cannon was out of place because no gun had been fired in Birmingham during the Civil War. But it had been cast for the Confederacy by Cassie's great-grandfather, and the Fairchilds had had it placed there.

The cannon was set on a concrete platform behind a curving stone parapet, more medieval than nineteenth-century, jutting from the face of the mountain like a forgotten soldier's outpost. As I approached, the deserted parapet was all I saw. But when I was past it, I looked again and this time there was a slender figure, a sudden apparition standing with its back to me against the stone wall. I gripped the steering wheel, braking hard, as if the car were balancing on the edge of the mountain. I realized that I was holding my breath. It was the same feeling I had had at Highlands the night I thought I saw the ghost. The same quick yearning, the same presentiment of loss. Except that this was real, this was Cassie.

I steadied myself and got out of the car.

"I've been looking all over for you," I said.

Cassie didn't look at me at first. When she turned her head, I saw she had been crying.

"Come get in the car. We'll go for a ride."

"I don't want to see you. You remind me of things."

"What things?" I said.

"Good things. Beautiful things. Things I don't want to have to remember."

She suddenly turned her back to me and climbed up on the muzzle of the cannon, sitting like a child on a park bench, legs dangling down in front of her.

Climbing up there seemed to soothe her. "Let's get out of here," I said.

She shook her head. "I like it. I used to climb up here sometimes when I was little — after one of Mother and Daddy's fights. Timmy would come along, too, but he was afraid to climb out far. He'd watch from there." She pointed to where I stood. "Sometimes he'd dare me to jump."

"It's a long way down."

"It doesn't feel that far. You have a wonderful sense of freedom for an instant — you've kicked free of everything. But it's too short to last."

"Are you trying to tell me that you've jumped off there."

"I was ten years old. I don't really remember whether I jumped or fell. It was right there." She pointed out to the left where I could see nothing but the mountain dropping off beneath her, a few trees gripping the side of it, and a tangle of underbrush below.

"I fell about fifteen feet. A pine tree broke my fall. Timmy ran home. Daddy came down and picked me up and carried me in his arms. The doctors said I was lucky. I had scratches over every inch of me and a concussion, but no broken bones. They said an adult wouldn't have survived."

She was silent, her expression brooding and faraway.

"Cassie. Come down. Please."

"Aren't you going to dare me to jump again? Don't you want me to jump?"

"It's Nick," I said. "Nick."

"Yes, it's Nick," she said. "But Timmy wants me to jump. They all do."

"What do you mean?"

"Uncle Asa thinks I should go away — until all this is over. He thinks I'm dangerous. Do you think I'm dangerous, Nick?"

"I love you," I said. "I don't want you to get hurt."

She just looked at me for a minute. Then she said, "Dear sweet Nick. The incurable romantic." She reached down and put her hands around my neck and kissed me. "Maybe I'll see you in Frisco sometime."

I became suddenly aware that we were not alone. I turned around. A limousine had pulled silently up behind me. It sat motionless, its long dark hulk blotting out what remained of the afternoon light. The rear door opened. Framed in the doorway was a slight figure in a black suit sitting stiffly like a doll, staring straight ahead. Without turning to look at us, he stretched out his arm, his small birdlike fingers beckoning to Cassie.

Cassie gave a low gasp that sounded like a whispered scream. Then she swung her legs around and in one movement, quick and clean as a gymnast, dropped down on the other side of the parapet, balancing on a narrow stone ledge that jutted out beneath the cannon.

Almost at the same second the front door of the car opened, and a large man in a chauffeur's uniform headed toward us.

"If you come one step closer, I'll jump," she said. "I swear I will."

The chauffeur stopped for an instant. He was close enough so that I could see his pockmarked face, the broad flat nose like an ex-boxer's. He looked back to the car. Asa Hammer lifted his hand and made a short jabbing gesture. Then the chauffeur was moving again, covering the space between us in a few big strides.

"Hold on," I yelled to Cassie. "I'm coming after you."

I swung my leg over the cannon and crawled out along the gun muzzle, sliding myself forward. Through my pants I could feel the old iron, cold and unforgiving. I had come almost far enough to reach out and touch her. Suddenly Cassie raised her hand, palm open, as if she were either greeting me or telling me to stop. I kept moving toward her. She looked at me with a cornered look. It was replaced by a secret smile, like a child who is playing a game no one else knows the rules to. For just a second she reminded me of her brother in that one unguarded moment last night. Then she was Cassie again, beautiful and unfathomable as ever, leaning back very slowly, drawing herself away, inch by inch, to some distant point where no one could follow.

I lunged for her, catching hold of her around the hips. Her body turned in my hands. I grabbed the inside of one leg and her buttocks and held on. But she was slipping through me as if a stronger hand than mine was pulling against me.

I felt pure empty space as Cassie fell away from me, as if everything had emptied out of me also. Then the emptiness began to reel and I kicked out, losing my balance, turning inside it. The whole world turning into a deep well of panicky darkness.

twenty-three

When I came around, I was lying on my back staring at a flat blank ceiling, the room around me one clean white unbroken wall. No sharp points. No hard edges. No sudden shout or cry to punctuate the still surface.

Amid the emptiness, I had found a bottom. But now I lay at a strange unmoving angle, suspended in a steady white daze that seemed unending. Out of it people came and went, hovered about me, left me alone.

A doctor in a white coat stepped up to the bed. My left leg was in traction, he said, broken in two places, bone piercing the skin in one of them. And I had a punctured lung. I would heal, he told me, but slowly. The limp would disappear with time. I had been lucky, he added. A tree had broken my fall.

Cassie's pine tree, I thought. The doctor was gone before I could move. But I grabbed the nurse's arm. "There was a girl with me," I said, "in the — accident with me. Where is she? What happened to her?"

The nurse looked at me as if I were still delirious. Maybe I was. I sank into a hot pillowed sleep, searching for the well of panic and emptiness that could lead me to Cassie.

*   *   *

The next time I opened my eyes bright sunlight was streaming through the thin gauze curtains over the window beside the bed. I wasn't sure whether I'd slept for a day or a week. But the white daze was beginning to lift. I squinted up at the familiar face standing above me.

"Hello, love."

"How long have I been here?" I asked.

"Five days," Melissa replied.

"They won't tell me what happened," I said. "Where is Cassie? Why won't someone tell me? Is she dead?"

"Dead?" Melissa exclaimed. "Of course not, love."

"What do you mean?" I said, lifting my head. "Where is she?"

"She's away — back east."

I looked at her without comprehending.

"The day after you fell. Her father sent her off."

"The day after I fell," I repeated. "I thought she fell, too. I was afraid she was dead."

Melissa smiled slightly. "You should have paid less attention to Cassie's balance and more to your own."

"What happened?"

"Two little boys were playing up there; they saw you fall. But it's hard to make much sense out of what they said."

"Tell me."

They had seen Cassie and me on the parapet, the big black car drive up, a man get out wearing a uniform like a policeman's only he wasn't. They had watched Cassie climb out where they knew it was dangerous and then I climbed out after her. They saw me grab for her and lose my balance. At the same time they watched the man in the uniform step out on the ledge from the other side, catch hold of her, and pull her back in.

"It frightened them when you fell," Melissa said. "They watched the car take Cassie away. Then they ran."

"How did I get here?" I asked.

"The father of one of the boys called the police. They said a woman had already called," Melissa said. "She didn't give her name."

I studied Melissa's face. "Does Cassie know I'm here?"

"I tried to reach her for four days, but they wouldn't put her on the line. Then last night about two AM she called."

"How is she?"

"She couldn't talk long. I told her you were going to be all right."

"What did she say?"

"She sounded relieved," Melissa said looking away from me. "I think they're keeping her pretty doped up."

I didn't say anything.

"I believe she really cares about you," she added. "She would have loved you if she could."

I nodded. "I guess I was supposed to be the fall guy all along," I said thickly.

I thanked Melissa for coming.

"Don't thank me, love," she replied. "I like to visit hospitals. The sight of someone in worse shape than I am always lifts my spirits."

A few days after that Hurlbut came to see me.

"How you feeling?"

"Better," I said.

"Better than who?" he asked.

I asked him how things were at the paper.

He said everything was fine. Walsh was working on his Ronald Reagan impersonation. "McDermott wants to know when you're gonna be back. I believe he actually misses you. Either that or he's tired of taking obits himself."

I told him I didn't know when.

Before he left he said, "I brought you a newspaper. Thought you'd like to keep up."

Hurlbut left the *Examiner* lying face down on the chair, just out of reach. When the nurse brought my dinner, I asked her to hand the paper to me.

There was a story by Mike Stankey on the front page. It was not a long story. It merely said that Wesley Waddell had been found dead in his cell. A heroin overdose.

The sheriff's deputy who was on duty said he didn't know how Waddell had come by the drug, but what with the money and manpower shortages, they couldn't watch him all the time. The district attorney said: "An addict is the cleverest person in the world when it comes to getting hold of what he needs. You could blindfold him and handcuff him to your leg and he'd still find a way."

I put the paper down. The twisted angle of my leg had begun to throb and I lay back and tried to relax.

Ten days later I walked out of the hospital on a pair of steel crutches, and as I swung through the sliding glass doors, the metal poles glinted in the sunlight. The day was bright and cold and clear. The kind of day to begin a journey to a place you'd never been.

Melissa had left my Chevrolet in the parking lot. I dug an old road map out of the glove compartment and spread it out on the seat beside me. To the west was the Louisiana bayou, Texas, and farther, off the map, California. Up east, beyond the big cities, somewhere on a dark Maine seashore perhaps, was Cassie.

When I left New York nearly two years ago, I had thought coming south meant coming home. Now there was not much farther south to go. Two hundred miles of rolling Alabama hills that flattened into dark sandy earth before hitting ocean.

I bent low over the map, closer to where I'd started, tracing the delicate blue veins of rivers, putting names to places I would have to learn to see all over again.

At last I found what I was looking for. A place where there would be deep woods, filled with wild magnolia and hemlock. Woods you could lose yourself in. A small still point on the map that had to be Frisco.